The Mythmaker

Mary Harrell

PUBLISHED BY CHIRON PUBLICATIONS

www.ChironPublications.com

Interior and cover design by Danijela Mijailovic
Printed primarily in the United States of America

ISBN 978-1-63051-500-3 paperback
ISBN 978-1-63051-501-0 hardcover
ISBN 978-1-63051-502-7 electronic
ISBN 978-1-63051-503-4 limited edition paperback

Library of Congress Cataloging-in-Publication Data
Names: Harrell, Mary, author.
Title: The mythmaker / by Mary Harrell.
Description: Asheville, N.C. : Chiron Publications, [2018] |
Summary: Follows Katie, the second of seven children, from
1962-65 when she is aged thirteen to seventeen, as she deals
with the loss and healing surrounding her mother's death.
Identifiers: LCCN 2018000786| ISBN 9781630515003
(pbk. : alk. paper) | ISBN 9781630515010 (hardcover : alk. paper)
Subjects: | CYAC: Coming of age--Fiction. | Death--Fiction. |
Mothers and daughters--Fiction. | Single-parent families--Fiction.
| Angels--Fiction.| Family life--Pennsylvania--Fiction. |
Pennsylvania--History--20th century--Fiction.
Classification: LCC PZ7.1.H3735 My 2018 | DDC [Fic]--dc23
LC record available at https://lccn.loc.gov/2018000786

To
my mother, Josephine Zardecki Stemrich
in whose loving memory I dedicate this healing myth.

To
young people everywhere
who navigate childhood without one or both of their parents.

Acknowledgments

I owe much gratitude to Chiron Publications, my gorgeous publishing team, for encouraging me to write *The Mythmaker*. I'm indebted to Len Cruz for his trustworthy editing suggestions and early excitement at my wish to write Katie's story. I couldn't have asked for better copy editors than Ron Madden and Shelby Voss who read every word with keen eyes and open hearts. I owe much gratitude to Danijela Mijailovic for her patience and skill at working with me until *The Mythmaker*'s evocative cover emerged; her decisions about the cover design and typsetting were perfect in every way. In Jennifer Fitzgerald, I found a true partner and editor who was with me every step of the way, always positive, encouraging, and ever so wise. Jennifer's professional sensibility helped me tell *The Mythmaker* as it should be told. Her support and expertise, from the most important early developmental decisions to the tiniest detail were essential, and I cannot thank her enough. It was from the Chiron Publications team that the idea to form a teen focus group emerged.

The following teen focus group members were clear from the start in saying exactly what type of cover image would or would not work for them as readers! From their able and varying opinions, a lively theme emerged. Each one of them is precious to me and I hope they are happy with our final choice. I offer humble gratitude to Saila Buser, Celia Clark, Sianna Berrio, Laila Kanaana, and Ella Briggs. Mixed media artist Cynthia Clabough, and *The Unseen Partner* author

Diana Croft contributed valuable ideas and much patience as our team moved toward a perfect conclusion.

Of my writing sisters who faithfully sit at my side each month providing wise guidance, I am simply and happily in their debt. They know that it's only fun to write, when it's fun to write. For those more difficult times, it's essential to hear the encouraging words, "Keep going." It is enough for me to know that every "next" writing meeting is around the corner, and if I want attention, I have to write. That's our deal. I acknowledge that the simplicity and dependability of our relationship is a great gift. To my brilliant and accomplished writing group, I humbly say, "Thank you for your contribution to each and every word of this book." Jean Ann, Barbara Beyerbach, Bonita Hampton, Sharon Kane, Tania Ramalho, Roberta Schnorr, and Chris Walsh you are my treasures.

Though I admit to the possibility of unwittingly leaving out some valuable contributors who read early drafts and shared their wisdom, I want to especially thank Diane Croft who chose to offer wise counsel, carefully seeking permission first, wondering if this or that might be helpful as an idea, or possibility. It always was. I am wild with happiness that her writing of the exquisite *The Unseen Partner* brought us to this path of collaboration. Sharon Kane read every word of my manuscript, more than once. I am grateful for her occasional calls to give patient lessons on punctuation, homonyms, homophones, homographs, and heteronyms; though I am a slow student she never gives up on me, saving me from missteps that authors should avoid. She is a leading national voice in the field of young adult literature and offered much that improved the book. I'm thankful too, that her ever-active mind unfailingly spins plans to make sure *The*

Mythmaker is in the hands and minds of people who know the field and might champion it along the way.

I am aware too, that remarkable teachers and mentors have blessed me with their presence, each, offering something precious until the poetics of my personal myth emerged. Though I didn't know it at the time, they were holding a transformative container, in which the threads winding through my life began to cohere. Tom Schur, a family systems therapist and social worker walked with me as I journeyed through the final stages of personal healing. For many years, I have not been in the physical presence of Phenomenologist and poet Robert Romanyshyn, or professor of Jungian Psychotherapy and Imaginal Psychology Veronica Goodchild, both emeritae professors at Pacifica Graduate Institute. Still, they continue to support my deepening understanding as an author and imaginal psychologist in the world. It is no surprise to me, that their guidance in dreams, email communications, and extraordinary ongoing work in the world, continues to bring me closer to my own vocation as a writer. It is my view, that Robert, Veronica and I are linked, as we greet the world with an intuitive sensibility, responding to whispers of love from a realm beyond time and space. I had the good fortune to meet core faculty member Dennis Patrick Slattery at a Pacifica Graduate Institute event in 2016. I was intrigued by Dennis' groundbreaking work on personal mythmaking. His understanding of myth as both a fiction, and a recurring act of re-membering allowed me to find the deeper truth in Katie Neumann's story (and my own).

My siblings and I share a history that binds us forever, and still, I don't expect that my own re-imagined past is entirely theirs. I take full responsibility for every memory I've mined to tell the story of Katie's life, as well as for the act of imagination that brought Katie's story to its enchanted ending. To JoAnn Stoudt, Jim Stemrich (who guides us all from another place), John David Stemrich, Michelle Stanton, Joseph Stemrich, and Marella Gregory I am indebted to you for your many acts of love and forgiveness. You've made of your lives what our mother would have wished. Please know that I claim this work as a fiction, based on the irrefutable fact we all shared: in 1962, our mother died and left us without her physical presence and unique loving heart. After that, any resemblance to Katie Neumann's life and our own is a result of authorly decisions, or my own interpretations of what was.

The genesis of Katie's story began many decades ago. I don't believe I could have written *The Mythmaker* if after my mother's death my uncles and aunts did not remain in my life, simply loving me. Though their love did not, could not, bring my mother back, it did prevent my joy from being swallowed by loss. Aunt Tina made sure I had dresses for proms and college dances, and a beautiful wedding gown that made me know that mother love can come in many forms. Aunt Gloria and Uncle Gil welcomed me into their home one wonderful summer, providing the only place where I had no chores or responsibilities. This kindness reminded me that life holds many surprises. During my first summer after high school graduation, I was a pre-college working girl. I lived with Aunt Madelyn and Uncle Harris in Arlington, Virginia, and was required by them to ante up $25 of each $50's of weekly salary for room and board. As a point of interest, I sold maids uniforms at Woody's Department Store in

Washington, D.C. Of my $25 weekly obligation, there was no discussion. No negotiation. No complaining. On the day I was delivered back home to pack for college, Aunt Madelyn handed me a bulging envelope. I gasped at realizing that she had given me the astounding gift of every dollar I had paid, a gigantic savings account for books, fees, and living expenses. This, after Aunt Madelyn surprised me with a shopping spree just weeks before I left her home; she was a stylish woman who knew about the best clothing, the 'good' brands and the magical shops that, in her view should make her niece's fashion statement. I modeled for her. She filled my shopping bags. Her bountiful act became my assurance that the irrational shame of being a motherless girl—my secret identity—didn't follow me to college. Uncles Patrick, Bobby, Ray, Carl, and Don were always generous with their pride in me, freely offering advice and support, and somehow knowing when one was needed, but not the other. There were others in our large family who made us know that we belonged to them. I'm grateful to them all.

To my daughter Lauren Fortgang, your talent and knowledge as a performer and voice-over artist has been invaluable to me through the writing of this book. You have been at my side with honest and loving feedback and buckets of encouragement. Always, you are the bright light in my world, my touch of magic and my proof that life is very good. To my tiny son James Michael, I write, as always, out of loving dedication to your unlived life, and wish to publicly acknowledge the waves of inspiration that your imaginal presence showers upon me. Dear husband Stephen, I am free to write each day because your generous heart allows me space to grow, and provides a loving home in which to create.

You run interference so that my dreams and passions might find expression in the world. At the end of the day, I am most grateful for those special evenings when we sing and dance together, a tender pastime that makes me want to write stories for others to hear.

Table of Contents

Soul asks that we embody her becoming
singing iterations of her low-sung song.
Unfamiliar figures gather, wordless witnesses
claiming notice in the crooked road of dreams.

— Mary Harrell

Chapter 1

We Won't Have a Circus   1962

If you lived through everything that happened on that Good Friday—which is about the holiest day of the year because Jesus was crucified—you might not remember *every* detail.

But you *would* see the Monday of your mother's funeral like a film clip ... playing over and over.

It starts with everyone sitting in rows of chairs, facing your mother's casket, in the funeral parlor. The priest would come in to say the Rosary. Everyone would know to leave the room very quietly, when the Rosary was over, taking a last stop at the casket to look at your mother.

There's Mr. Schu, who owns the drug store in Wilkes-Barre. He would have known your mother in a special way. She kept everything together at the drug store—by sitting up in the balcony, looking down at the customers ... and, doing the books for him.

She did that, even though your father was angry, saying more than once, "I can take care of my *own* family."

Mr. Schu would move—bent and slow—even though he usually doesn't do that. You can hear him saying something (softly) to your mother, before he touches her hand and leaves. It would be so strange to think, that you, and your brothers and sisters, and aunts and uncles and cousins aren't the only people who are sad.

When everyone leaves, it's a surprise that the gentle and serious funeral director looks straight at you, extending his hand toward the casket, and tells you and your brothers and sisters to come up to stand around your mother. First, he would have Andrew come up, followed by Olivia Marie and Evan, then John Conner.

If you were me, you and Sofia would be called up last, because you both (being thirteen, and fifteen) would be the oldest. The funeral director would say to each one of you (when you came up), "It's OK for you to touch your mother."

"If you want to … you can give her a kiss," he added.

I remember noticing that your hands looked beautiful, no longer having those blue veins that popped up sometimes. They were white and looked very soft. I touched them and knew in a new way…

that you weren't living anymore.

Your hands … were as hard and cold as frozen ground. Even with that, I still liked that they looked so beautiful. And I knew I wanted to kiss your face, even though I knew, it would be cold and hard too.

I wasn't going to miss that kiss for anything.

Sofia had tears running down her cheeks when she told you, "I love you."

We all had tears going down our faces. I appreciated so much that no one was there, not even Daddy, when we all watched Sofia take the lace mantilla from around the sides of your hair, and cover your face with it.

If you were watching us, you would have been so proud of ... how much we loved you. You would have thought (like I did) that we were lucky to have a good leader for a sister. Sofia was making sure your face would be protected after you were buried. She always knows what to do.

I think of that—standing around your casket—all the time. It was the last time that we were with you, looking at you. It was the last time we could do ... anything for you. We couldn't protect your face or kiss you, after that day.

I liked that we got to do it, because it was impossible to believe, in the days and weeks and months after that, that you were dead—that you couldn't come back to us if you tried.

Seeing you that day. Feeling your cold face, and hands, helped us know— no matter how sad we were, nothing could bring you back.

We all got in black cars that took us through Ashley. We passed Cook Street, and the colliery ... on to Sugar Notch, and finally, to Holy Family Church. I remember, as we approached the church, there were yellow school buses parked, on the side of the street.

That seemed crazy. Since when did school buses show up at funerals? Cars filled the parking lot beside the church. There were so many. I didn't know what to think.

17

The next thing I knew, Sofia, John Conner, Evan and I were standing behind Daddy at the back of the church. He held Andrew in his right arm, on his other side he held Olivia Marie's hand.

We all wore the Easter clothes Daddy bought for us when you were in the hospital. I wore my red Jackie Kennedy pillbox hat, with my black and white tweed suit, just like I showed you last Wednesday. Sophia made sure the boys wore suits and clip-on ties. With spotless white gloves and brand new dresses, Sophia and Olivia Marie looked like girls whose mother fussed over them all morning.

All of a sudden, the organ music changed, from a murmur, to a blast.

Everyone in the church stood up, at the same time, turning to look at us. When they stood, it sounded like thunder.

All those people—the kids from St. Leo's School the nuns, all our relatives, the whole town.

That was the first time I knew, firsthand, that something could be terrible because it was too big for you. And, at the same time, be full of sadness for hundreds of people. Daddy turned to me, Sofia, John Conner and Evan …

He said, "We won't have a circus— there won't be any crying."

We all nodded. Daddy turned around, and the seven of us (Izzie was still in the hospital) walked up the middle aisle. We had to pass your casket, before taking our seats next to you.

Aunt Agnes sang the 'Ave Maria,' and the 'Panis Angelicus'. You wouldn't believe how beautiful it was. The problem was, I kept remembering that you were in the metal casket on our left, close to the altar.

I kept remembering that you always sang those songs at other people's funerals or weddings. Now, your voice was stuck with you in the casket.

Every time I thought of that—you in the casket—a cry, a huge cry, tried to explode from my throat.

I'll never know for sure, if it would have been a cry. A scream. A loud moan. Or a loud word, like "Mommy!" because ... I held it in every time, until my throat ached with the pressure of it.

I didn't want to disappoint Daddy and have a circus. So, each time (maybe twice a minute) the sadness tried to come out, I would keep it in. That's pretty much all I did during your service—work to keep myself from being a circus.

My mind and eyes weren't helping.

My mind repeated over and over, "A mother is supposed to go to the hospital to have a baby and then come home." I couldn't understand why that simple thing didn't happen. I couldn't make my mind accept that you went into shock and died two hours after Izzie was born. I knew that couldn't be possible, and at the same time, it was exactly what happened.

My eyes kept reminding me that you were in that casket.

We always had you beside us: at the dinner table, when we opened the Christmas presents, and at our birthday parties.

You were beside us when we went for rides to the Alaskan Freeze in the summers, singing 'Good Night Irene,' or 'How Much Is that Doggie in the Window,' or 'I've Been Working on the Railroad.'

We always had you up in the choir at church, but this was the first time we had you beside us in a casket, right in front of the altar. That's why I kept needing to cry.

Chapter 2

Got Me Over a Barrel   1964

Mom, when I was in my bed last night, a lady...

A lady ... appeared.

When she first showed up, I couldn't see her.

That's right. I couldn't see her. If you want to know how I knew she was there without seeing her, I don't have an answer.

That's not all...

I know that the rest of this story might sound totally made up. Some of it might even seem funny. But I promise you, if it happened to you, you wouldn't think so.

This lady started to come towards me. When she did ... she started to have a body! It wasn't like, first she didn't have one but then she did.

It was that her body started showing up, little by little. There were tiny, moving pieces that seemed to vibrate, and these tiny pieces began taking on the shape of a face, then a body.

A body that looked like I could stick my finger right through it.

It felt like she was, maybe, a ghost of someone I didn't know. The weird thing is that she seemed to know me. It was as if she came especially to give me a small box that she held in her hand. A present.

All I know is that I wanted her, needed her, to go away.

I remember thinking, "I can't have a ghost showing up in my bedroom, especially now." Everything, including me, feels wrong without you. It's been two whole years since you left us. Things never got back to normal, whatever that's supposed to mean...

I'm more scared than anything. I hate that the lady brought me a present. Who would want a present from a ghost?

At first, I was so afraid that I couldn't even move. Not my foot. Not my finger—nothing.

My heart was beating so loud that I thought it might explode. I was a rabbit whose heart could pop out and kill her.

When I finally thought to jump out of bed, somehow, thinking this would help—like breaking a spell, I was horrified to discover, that I still couldn't move.

I thought, "I'm trapped in a horror movie."

Knowing that giving up wasn't even a choice, I used all my strength, to jump, determined to escape. Somehow, there I was—upright—running for my life.

The worst thing is, that even though I was going as fast as I could, I figured out, pretty soon, that I wasn't moving at all.

Not an inch.

Some very brave part of me kept saying, "Think! Think!"

It was then that I noticed that the floor was actually moving under me. (This is the part where someone might think this is supposed to be a funny story.) No matter how hard I ran, it was as if I was running on a big barrel, with the barrel spinning underneath. I was actually running like crazy, yet staying in the same place.

That was when I had the idea that if running wouldn't work, I could leap to Sofia's bed—two feet away. To my relief, I did leap. The next thing I knew, I was hugging her tight.

She never woke up. That was for the best. By then, I was sweating a lot. (She might have said that I couldn't stay—being wet and all). I really believe that hugging Sofia is what made the lady disappear.

Without you, I feel like I'm a bug, something that's small and unpleasant. Something that doesn't belong with people.

And now, I'm a wacko who has a ghost showing up.

If you have any suggestions I'm completely willing to overlook the fact that I haven't had one idea from you since you died.

Two years had gone by, between the day my mother left us, and the night my ghost showed up in my bedroom. When your mother dies, you're not usually going to hear from her again.

But some unusual thing *did* happen—a simple and *new* thought kept coming into my head.

It replaced the thought that "no one knows what it's like to be a girl who doesn't have her mother—"

That, "not having a mother is an embarrassing situation."

That, "the person who's supposed to be in your corner–isn't."

That, "your mom's not helping you become a teenager."

And that, "no one's sitting in a chair when you come home from school for you to kneel beside and rest your head on."

The new thought is barely there, like a nighttime fog that you hardly notice. It goes something like this:

"You're loved."

It doesn't completely make sense.

To call it a *complete* idea is even stretching it.

Sometimes it comes like a tiny whisper—

"You're loved."

Sometimes it comes like a warm feeling in my body—

"You're loved."

And sometimes, it's something more altogether. But that's all I can say, because I don't really have words to explain the "something more."

Then, in the middle of my getting almost comfortable with the idea that I was loved, maybe that I belonged in the world in a very new way, everything changed forever.

But before the ghost showed up, so much happened—two years' worth of this-is-your-life-if-your-mother-dies. To skip over any of it would be to skip the part that nobody tells you about.

So, I'll just back up, then you'll know everything.

And the rest of the story will make complete sense.

Chapter 3

Good Friday   1962

When Daddy came home from the hospital on that Good Friday, he walked through the parlor like a puppet whose strings weren't being pulled by anyone. It was as if a puppeteer had fallen asleep in the middle of a show. Daddy's head hung low, his shoulders sagging. The way he walked was more like the hunchback of Notre Dame than our father.

He didn't seem worried or rushed like when he left the house earlier. He took heavy steps across the room but didn't look at any of us.

I already knew you were dead, because when the phone rang hours before, Grandma Aelish must have picked it up because I heard her screaming from the next room. When I ran in to see what was going on, I saw her on her knees with her head down. The phone was on the floor beside her.

She seemed to cry and scream at the same time, saying, "Not Julia. Take ME instead." She said that over and over, and I just stood there, frozen.

Just between you and me, I didn't think Grandma meant that.

I thought, "There she is again, needing to be the center of attention." I'm a little bit older now, and I know I might have been kind of hard on her.

I could hear John Conner upstairs in his bedroom, shouting over and over, "No. No. No. No. No. No. No." A loud bang sounded with each "No."

He must have figured out on his own, like I did, what happened.

When I ran to John Conner's room, I saw him banging his head. He was hitting it (hard) against the bedroom wall. Maybe I put my arms around him, since I was 13, and he was 12. I might have done that, but maybe I just stood there not knowing what to do.

Without you there, or Daddy, and Grandma downstairs screaming, it was so creepy, and scary. It all seemed to hurt somewhere new and deep.

And yet, instead of only feeling hurt or scared I remember having an idea: "Somebody should tell the kids." I felt a little stronger, and more grown-up, thinking that way. So, I went to check on Andrew. He was standing in his crib in his diaper, holding an empty bottle, looking confused. I figured he was safe enough. The only one in the house who wasn't acting crazy. So, I left him there and went down the street looking for Evan.

He was playing with Tommy Terasavage, up in a tree.

I yelled at him, "You have to come down and go home, Mommy died."

I'm really sorry I told him about you like that. He told me later that the way I yelled it—to him up in the tree—stayed inside him for a long time. He said it made it worse, that you shouldn't say that to a six-year-old kid. Anyway, I took him by the hand and brought him home.

When we got to our house a few minutes later, Olivia Marie was running around a bush in the front yard. Her arms were swinging, and she had on a skirt that opened like a parachute as she spun. She was smiling that sweet smile of hers. And even with everything going on, I thought that her face was like a little angel.

With my free hand, I brought her from the yard to the porch, and into the house. She was so happy that I didn't even tell her about you until we were inside.

I can't exactly remember where Sofia was. If she was there, she would have been in charge, doing everything I did that day. Grandma was on the phone, making sure our relatives knew. I guess that's how people knew to come to your funeral on Monday.

We all just quietly walked around the house or sat, like you do when something bad just happened and you know the best thing to do is nothing. You're too scared to throw a ball, or to swing in the back yard, or to play back scratching games up on the bed.

That Friday was the only time I can ever remember when all of us were quiet. It was the only time I could remember not thinking up things to do, like being builders and putting a few nails in the side of the house, or roller skating, or running from the back porch to the swing set, jumping on the swing, swinging high very fast, then jumping off and running to the back porch to do it again.

It felt right to not move, to not talk, and to not think of anything whatsoever.

By the time Daddy came home and walked through the parlor, we already knew the worst part of what happened. When he reached the archway between the parlor and the dining room, he leaned against the framed opening. That was when he made himself turn and look at us.

He said the strangest thing, like he was talking to the air, "She was just a kid."

He was talking about you! Like you weren't our mother. Like you were somebody only he knew. So, on top of you being dead, he was talking about another kind of you. A "young" you.

I thought you were pretty old, being our mother and all. And I didn't appreciate him talking that way. I know he didn't mean anything by it, but he was making things more creepy than they already were.

I don't remember seeing him again that day, but around 4 o'clock Sofia and I found money in a jar and decided to take the kids to Good Friday services and then to eat. We walked to St. Leo's, all of us.

Nobody talked to us, but people were staring, which was a surprise. We didn't think the whole town knew about the hospital and what happened to you. I was proud of us, that we knew to go to the Good Friday services.

On the way back, Sofia and I took the kids to Taganani's Pizza Parlor. Nobody even told us to do that. And you'll be happy to know that the kids didn't act up or get in any kind of trouble. I think Sofia carried Andrew most of the way. Izzie was still in the hospital, until after the funeral. We made sure everybody was clean. So you don't need to worry about that.

Chapter 4

An Angel or a Ghost?   1964

On the night of the ghost lady's second visit I was less afraid—not so freaked out—when her body started to become visible. I knew that the *you are loved* idea wasn't an idea at all. It wasn't even a feeling now.

It was *her*. I was loved because *she* was with me.

If you're thinking that the lady was my mother, you'd be wrong.

We began speaking in thoughts, not regular words.

She said, "You need to know that you shouldn't mistake an angel for a ghost." With that she smiled, her soft eyes looking right at me. She took a small step toward me, but I jumped back. As if we were doing a little dance, she stepped away and smiled again.

I liked that. Even though I wasn't as afraid as the first time she showed up, I liked that she could take a hint.

"Who are you?" I asked. This speaking without using words was like reading each other's minds.

"You can think of me as a messenger," she said.

If you were in the room with us, if you could hear her, you'd know that her voice was very tender like my mother's voice, and yet it wasn't my mother at all.

You'd know that she was calm, and liked to pay attention to me, like my mother did when I had a frightening dream. You'd know that if I could let her touch me—which I wouldn't—her touch would be like light.

It would be there but wouldn't have weight.

Somehow I found the nerve to ask, "If you're a messenger, why are you acting like a ghost?"

"What do you mean? I'm not swooping around the room. I'm standing here. And you're standing beside your bed."

I didn't say anything, but I didn't look away.

"I'm a unique kind of messenger, one that doesn't have a body like you do. In the far-away place where my people are, we call my being a *subtle body*.

"Is that why you said that I shouldn't mistake an angel for a ghost?"

I also wondered, but didn't say, that this subtle body idea might have something to do with my ability to put my finger right through her—if I were brave enough.

"Yes." She said. The distinction between angels and ghosts seemed to hold some meaning for her but for me—

I'm not quite sure.

"Are you an angel?"

"You could call me that."

34

"I see your body and face, and the last time you came I noticed that you had a small box for me. You're wearing a long robe, like the one on the statue of the Blessed Virgin Mary over there ... on my dresser," I said. Now, more confused than frightened.

She turned toward the dresser, then back to me, "I thought you would like that. You see, I'm here when you say your prayers. You seem calm then. It reminds me of you, *before* everything changed..."

"You've been here more than the first time I saw you?"

"Yes, I've been with you for a very long time."

Thinking about all of this, I hoped that she didn't try to give me that box.

Because she knew more than I did about what was going on she said, "You don't need to worry about the box. I'll talk with you instead of giving it to you, if that's OK with you."

Now, she's the one who's waiting.

"Where is it?" I asked.

"It's here, but you can't see it."

"Why not?"

"It's a gift, but there are other ways to give it to you, other ways that won't make you afraid," she said.

"Like me talking with you?" I asked.

And with a "yes," tender as falling snow, her head bent a little, and she was gone.

It looks like I've gotten ahead of my story. Again.

It's true, that the lady—

my angel—*did* come back.

When she did, I wasn't as frightened as on the first night of our ... friendship.

Between April 20, 1962 and the night my angel *first* appeared two years later, I had to learn three lessons. Lessons I would've liked to wish out of existence— if there is such a thing.

I had to find out, the hard way, that there are things you don't get to decide, if you're a kid like me.

In the end, I did learn those lessons, and I gave each one its own name.

Lesson Number One, I called Brilliant Brain.

Lesson Number Two, The Vampire, and...

Lesson Number Three, The Crystal Coffin.

Chapter 5

Brilliant Brain   1963

It's Friday, April 19, 1963, exactly three hundred and sixty-four days since my mother died. I'm walking home from school, hunched over the usual load of books. Tomorrow, I'll haul them back to school. Taking them back and forth is the best I can do. I can't make myself open them or pay attention to what's inside. The one exception: English homework, which I love.

Sherry Prymus is with me as usual, but she might as well be invisible. I hardly notice her. Lately, we're not really interested in the same things. Don't get me wrong. I like walking with her because she doesn't talk too much. As we get closer to home she'll go left on Davis Street; I'll head straight to my house on Cook Street.

My stomach is churning, even though I feel flat as a pancake inside. I know that something's wrong. Today is different, but I can't put my finger on it. I notice that with each step, a bad feeling seems to grow.

Sherry asks, "I wonder if friends tell each other when they have problems?"

I don't say anything at first. It's as if some old guy has his boney claws wrapped around my intestines—squeezing the life out of them.

I know I'm supposed to say something. Sherry isn't fooling me with the question. We've talked a hundred times about how we're great friends. How we tell each other every secret. We've been friends since we were five, when we played at the dump after school like we were at Disneyland.

So I try.

"My mind moves around in circles. Random thoughts always find a connection to my mother being gone."

She doesn't say a word, but she's not running away either. I go on.

"Everything I think about is jagged, like I'm in a hallway that a clumsy guy walked through, bumping every picture. It's as if, every picture looks wrong instead of interesting."

Nothing, from Sherry.

A thought comes out of ... nowhere. This one I keep to myself, "I will *not* stand for one more day without my mother."

I say out loud, "When your mother dies it hurts worse than anything. After a while, it's supposed to get better. That's what people keep saying. I'm beginning to worry that they're big liars."

"I know exactly what you mean, I hate liars. My brother Mario's a liar—I also hate him because he called me fat last week."

I've said all I can for one day. But my conversation—with myself—doesn't stop: "The only people that feel better are those liars. They feel better each day. They don't have to feel like they have polio—their bones, twisting like crazy inside an iron lung. People don't understand that a person like me only *looks* normal."

I can't explain why that one thing—their not understanding—is the *worst* part for me, because ... I have no idea.

Sherry asks, "Do you think I'm fat?"

The answer comes easily, "No."

"Are you mad at me? She asks.

"No."

"See you tomorrow—unless you want me to come over to do homework later."

As she makes her left on Davis Street, I don't answer.

What's happening, as I head toward my own house, doesn't have a name yet. It's just there, lurking. I do know that two things are true.

One: A crazy maniac, the gut squeezer, has taken over my body.

Two: My stomach is blabbing, in the language of lurches and cramps, "Something is different today. And it's not good."

In the middle of this mess that happens to be my life, something good pops up, like a clown in a pop-goes-the-weasel box. I didn't expect this. Not today.

Have you ever had the experience where something brilliant, and new, shows up in your brain?

A big light bulb goes off and you say, "That's it!"

That's what's happening to me. I realize: It *will* be the end of the world if my mother doesn't come home—today. Right then, I get my genius idea—

The world could never be so mean, could never deny my need for my mother—today.

Exactly at that moment I hear, (from Genius Brain), "She *will* be home. Because you've reached the very end of your rope."

"The end of the line," Genius Brain adds.

Right there, I know: "Life is good. There *is* a God," even though, I admit still feeling sick in my stomach—a deeper part of me (which I'm ignoring) is saying, "Hold on there, Buckeroo!"

"Why didn't I realize this before, that something like this ... could actually happen?" I say to myself.

"Because," Genius Brain answers, "you can't have your mother back *until* you can't stand not to. Anyone who needs her mother as bad as you do, *has* to have her show up."

From Genius Brain, as if I'm just not too bright, "Heh, heh, heh ... If you hadn't been so brave, she would have come back last month—or earlier."

I don't mind the taunting. I'm beside myself with hope. The steps to my house, soon to become my house again, are only feet away.

Crashing through the door, I holler, "Mom!"

"MOM!" The smile on my face could light up an underground city.

Silence.

Running up the stairs, I'm thinking, "Of course, she's probably in her bedroom. That's the place where we say the family Rosary. Where I think she might actually *see* us."

But after I check her room, then two more … something, grabs my attention. It's that sick feeling in my body.

I notice something else—a lifeless something else—as still as a tree in winter. The only thing present is her absence.

Genius Brain, with his terrific idea—gone.

In his place is a mass of sorrow.

If you were me, you'd be back in your mother's room, on your mother's bed, crying and moaning.

This would be you, knowing in a brand new way that you will always be a motherless girl.

Something inside you had figured it out on the way home that day, probably the same part of you that caused your guts to squeeze 'til they hurt.

You could finally see your life, at least for now, clear as a bell.

Before your mother died, you'd be climbing, halfway up a sheer cliff called "growing up." You'd be having a blast, because your mother is your excellent guide. She's tethered to your side, like you need her to be. She's done this climb before, with *her* mother—your very cool Babcia (who died too). Not the grandmother you have to keep an eye on.

But now, you'd know that your mother has disappeared. Fallen off a crazy ledge. She's a thousand miles below … in a miserable pile of craggy rock.

By some mystery, you didn't fall with her.

You're left alone, too afraid to move toward the top, too paralyzed to go back down. You know with every muscle in your body, that the only way for you to keep going is for you to have a guide.

But you don't.

LESSON NUMBER ONE

You might reach a day when you miss your mother so much—you need her so much—that your brain will *really* tell you, "There's no way in the world, that she won't come back. Now."

But it won't be true.

Chapter 6

The Vampire   1963

It was in July of 1963, that my father married Eugenia.

Her face scares me because it looks angry, like she might say something mean any minute. A huge black space between her two front teeth looks like she lost a tooth. You can't even ignore it because she likes to say, "I have a diastema. It's a gap between two teeth." When she says the word diastema she sounds mad, but I don't know why. She distinctly pronounces every sound, as if it's especially important and she means to give you a test on it when she's done. If I were her, I wouldn't be bringing attention to it. Also, her nose looks too big for her face, like she put it on to disguise herself. She puts lipstick on way above the top of her upper lip. I keep thinking, "Why would anyone do that?"

Just looking at Eugenia makes me embarrassed and makes me miss my mother who was very small and pretty. And nice to people. Maybe, the way Eugenia looks wouldn't matter if she wasn't so mean.

My father said, "We'll call her Mother." Inside, I always call her Eugenia.

I asked her a simple question one day. Her answer (which I'm telling you about now) says all you need to know about her.

She'd been with us for about a month.

Our family moved that summer from Ashley, PA where we swam all day in Chester's Creek. We left a load of good stuff behind (Little Rezzy, and the woods where I had my secret grotto, to name two). After moving, Allentown's Cedar Crest Pool was the best we could do for swimming. Considering it was a city pool, it was okay.

I got used to some drawbacks. It was too crowded, too loud, and it didn't have "the woods" nearby, so you couldn't catch minnows or bake potatoes in a hole you dug. Those problems, I didn't get over. But there was a new one, which came with Daddy marrying Eugenia and us living close to Allentown's Cedar Crest Pool.

I was starting to get tired of taking the little kids to the pool for the whole day that summer, from Monday to Saturday, and giving them their baths every night, and doing the dishes and cleaning the house every Friday morning, before going to the pool with the kids.

To be fair, I didn't give the kids baths on Thursday night either, because I was allowed to babysit for Mrs. Arnold to earn money for school lunch. I also got to use the money for fabric, to make my wrap-around skirts, which I loved.

One day the thought came to me, "When you get a new mother, she's supposed to do a lot of the chores, like your real mother would do. You're supposed to go back to being a kid."

My real mother thought I was smart and amazing. Remembering this one fact gave me the courage to ask Eugenia for some teenage time at the pool with *only* my friends. I made my move one afternoon after bringing the kids back from swimming.

I figured that because she never had children before, it didn't cross her mind that a teenager shouldn't be doing so many things around the house. Or tons of babysitting. If you were me, you'd be thinking that *maybe* she didn't know that the mother is supposed to do most of those things.

So I asked, "Mother, (how hard it was to call her that), what if I took the kids to Cedar Crest *five* days a week, and on the sixth day, I went *alone* — so I could hang out with my friends?"

My idea seemed more than fair to me.

With a voice robbed directly from a witch in a fairy tale, Eugenia spun around and said, "They're not my responsibility, not my children, not my blood—*and neither are you.*"

I remember thinking, "Ew! Who says that kind of thing?"

I knew one thing for sure, that it wasn't that she didn't *know* what to do to be our mother, she didn't *want* to be our mother, because we weren't her "blood."

Mommy, you and daddy acted like you won the lottery when you got us kids. Daddy would always be in a great mood, telling stories and running behind our bikes holding on to the seat, not telling us that he had let go—that we were riding on our own! And he'd be cheering us on, and laughing, like nobody in the world but us could learn to ride a bike so fast.

45

You had Mrs. Kosenchack sew us dresses, so Sofia and I could dance in the Polish festival. I might have only been ten, but I remember everything—

Bright ribbons were stitched ten deep on the hems of our folk costumes. Yards more streamed from our hair like we were Shirley Temple. The night of the festival we had so much fun chasing each other up and down the stairs (at least until I stepped on Sofia's sash). When her festival dress ripped, you didn't even get mad. So I have no idea why all of a sudden, we're not kids who someone could like.

Grandma Aelish says terrible things to us too, but I don't mind when she says them. With her it's more like Grandma's just being herself. Even though she says awful things, it's easy to know that she loves us a lot. If you asked me how I know all of this, I'd just have to say, "I just know it—inside."

Grandma says we acted like wild animals when you were alive. Yesterday she came over and actually said, "You killed your mother and now you're killing your father!"

I don't believe her, but you should know that that happened.

I think Grandma meant, that when you were still with us, we ripped our dresses, and kept throwing the dodge ball into Mrs. Gallagher's yard. She might have been remembering that we got Patsy Cooney's eyelid caught with the fish hook. That we had to keep letting out the fishing line while we all ran down Cook Street, yelling.

I don't think she even knows that after a fight with Patsy Cooney, I put dog poop in a lunch bag and left it in front of the Cooney's front door. If she did find out somehow, then, I guess, I could see her point about us acting like wild animals.

But that's not what I'm even talking about.

I'm talking about that after how much you and daddy had fun with us—how could it be that now, we have to hear:

"You're not my blood."

"Isn't that disgusting, Mother?"

I miss being a kid who the mother likes.

I miss the back scratches you used to give me. I miss the times that you took me to Bingo and the way you'd open a Peppermint Patty, break it into five pieces and put it in the middle of the table for the ladies and me to share.

But I'm not saying all these things to complain, I'm talking to you because something very bad happened last night, the night Eugenia said the thing about we're not her blood. When I said my prayers, I was really mad, madder than I've been in my whole life. So I put my foot down.

I started screaming at God.

You heard me right...

at God.

I yelled, "You took my mother away, so you can bring her back. Bring her back right now! Not tomorrow. Tonight."

In my heart, I was really mean, and I didn't care that it was probably a sin to scream at Him.

"I don't even like you," I yelled.

"I hate you for taking our mother away, for causing Eugenia to come into our home. Acting like she's the boss."

"I hate you for giving Grandma a big mouth."

When I got off my knees and tucked myself in, I was afraid, mostly because I scared myself with all that yelling and carrying-on.

The next thing I knew I had this dream:

You're swooping over my head, like a vampire with huge bat wings, diving down—then swooping up—just before your bloody fangs hit my face.

Worst of all are your eyes.

They're blood red and empty—like they came from hell.

Your mouth is mean but a little bit scared, which worries me a lot. I wake up shaking all over. It's as if, anything might happen next, but nothing does.

So, I went back to sleep.

If I live to be a million years old, I'll never forget your eyes and teeth, and that swooping way you flew around the room.

I know that I started the whole thing. I shouldn't have tried to get rid of the kids one day a week. I shouldn't have thought that Eugenia could have better mother habits.

I know that I made the "vampire you" show up, Mommy.

Do you think you can forgive me for making you suffer like that, Mommy?

I'm mixed up, and nervous like you wouldn't believe. I do know one thing for sure, that I'll never, as long as I live, yell at God again. I'll never tell Him what to do. And no matter how lonely I get, I'll never demand that you turn up alive.

LESSON NUMBER TWO

You could reach a day, when you miss your mother *so much*, that you pick a fight with God. Even if you're holier than I was. Even if you never screamed at God before. You *still* could surprise yourself by getting so mad that your anger bursts out.

Chapter 7

The Crystal Coffin   1963

There's still one secret I have, and it's kind of connected to my needing you so much that I ended up screaming at God. I better spit it out now, because I'm wondering if I have to give it up along with everything else that's getting me in trouble.

You probably remember how much I used to love the Colored Fairy Books.

The Blue Fairy Book and The Green Fairy Book were my absolute favorites. I remember the story from The Green Fairy Book called, "The Crystal Coffin." The magician turned the brother into a stag and imprisoned the sleeping maiden in a glass coffin and enchanted all the lands around them.

That story has somehow turned into our life now.

Once upon a time we had you, with us. Our lives were full of wonder. We could walk in the woods, have secret grottos, climb the cliff to the frog pond ...

Then, the dark magic happened, and you died.

I also remember, the story had a baby horse, maybe a few minutes old, who was wobbling himself to a standing position for the first time, when BOOM. There he was, forever frozen, awkward and stuck in the middle of his first try. His mother stood beside him, proud and carefully watching.

But then, she got frozen, too.

Now, in our real life (like in the story) everything is frozen…

Everything is waiting for warmth—waiting for a magician more powerful than the one that enchanted it in the first place.

My secret, is that sometimes, you're not in the ground, but in a glass box—a crystal coffin—downstairs in the living room. We're all there with you, on Cook Street.

We keep you with us for as long as the enchantment lasts.

I don't really waste my time hoping that a magician calls you back to life.

I'm just so relieved that you're in that crystal case, in the living room. You look so beautiful.

Your hair is long and thick around your face.

Your cheeks and hands look soft. So white that I can almost see through them (reminding me of my subtle figure, my angel).

Your long dress is delicate like a blue butterfly's wing.

And on your feet, you wear satin slippers with tiny diamonds that glisten when the sun comes through the living room window.

Maybe I'm supposed to want you to be alive, and of course I do, that's why I was screaming at God. But mostly I know, that I will settle for you in a crystal box, just to see your face.

Sometimes, I have to blink away the whole thing. I tell myself that maybe ...

I only go there in my mind. I imagine seeing you—not a maiden—but you.

The truth is,

you really are at Cook Street. In the crystal coffin.

Is that too crazy? And if it is, should I stop believing it?

In one way, I hope you don't answer anytime soon, I'm not sure I could give up having you with me, in the crystal coffin.

In another way, I hope you do answer. I'm getting really tired inside, and sad, because of everything that's going on: Eugenia. Upset stomachs. The vampire you. The fight with God.

I really love the kids and I want to help you out by being a good big sister to them, but they're too much work.

I'm also worried because I can't figure out if I decide to go to the enchanted woods at Cook Street

or

if something takes me there without my permission.

LESSON NUMBER THREE

You might miss your mother *so much*, that you will accept getting her back *any* way you can, even if she has to be in a crystal coffin.

It wasn't long after I learned my three lessons, that my angel started visiting. You've already heard about the first time she showed up, and the second.

Pretty quickly after that, I began to suspect that my angel saw what was going on in my life. She *knew* everything. I wondered, could an angel *really* do that without me knowing about it?

I've heard—like everyone else has—that there's such a thing as a guardian angel. But just because a person hears that, or even believes it, doesn't mean an angel's going to show up in real life.

It's like questioning, "Do you believe in God?"

Even if the answer is, "Yes," you *do not* want Him showing up to have a talk with you. That only happens to people like Moses. And when it did happen to Moses, it just about killed him.

The answer to my suspicions about my angel knowing everything about me came a little bit at a time. I noticed that when I had a sad or angry situation to deal with—there she was.

Not always, but enough to think, "This probably isn't a coincidence."

Any doubts I might have had cleared up the day I stopped at Maura O'Hara's house before choir rehearsal.

Chapter 8

Isn't My Maura Beautiful?   1965

Maura O'Hara is in the 11th grade with me. We're kind of friends. Even though she's dating Andrew McCeever, we hang out after school sometimes, because I've joined the choir and so has she. Andrew McCeever hasn't.

If you're surprised that I'm actually allowed to be in the choir, well so am I! The reason for this change in my life is because my sister Sofia has come home.

I haven't mentioned that when dad married Eugenia and we all moved to Allentown, Sofia stayed for a year with Uncle Steve and Aunt Paula, so she could graduate from St. Leo's High School, in Ashley.

Now, a year later, she's with us again. It's Sofia who makes the biggest fuss on birthdays, like my mother used to do. She uses money from her Bell Telephone job to buy birthday presents for the kids, and beautiful cakes.

She makes the blowing-out-the-candles thing a big happy deal, saying, "You are special because you were born!"

Once in a while, on Friday nights (if Eugenia and my father don't have to grocery shop or go out with their friends the Elliot's and the Leonard's), Sofia and I—because we're not babysitting— go to dances at the YMCA or the Ag Hall. That's the Agricultural Hall.

She styles my hair in a long, teased flip. I wear a short tunic over bell bottoms, and when we get to the Ag, I take off the bell bottoms and stash them under the bleachers until the dance is over.

Between my beautiful long hair, my mini "dress," and my long legs, I look like a movie star—that's what Sofia says.

When I'm with Sofia, I'm not nervous. It doesn't matter that I'm shy, because Sofia always knows what to do. She's sassy with boys, so I let her do the talking and make all the decisions, which *usually* works out.

What's important about my high school career is that with Sofia being back home and helping with the younger kids after school—I get to be in the choir.

Maura and I are waiting for Sister Mary John to begin practicing "Wouldn't It Be Loverly," from *My Fair Lady*, which is a song that I love AND—like every other song on that album—I have it completely memorized. I wouldn't ordinarily be up on something like that except for my babysitting job with Mrs. Arnold, who I happen to *also* love.

I melted a bunch of albums—by accident—one Thursday night when I was taking care of Ann for the Arnold's. Neither Mr. nor Mrs. Arnold had mentioned to me that the top of the receiver box seriously heats up.

After I finished listening to each album, I thought it would work if I stacked them there—on the top of the receiver box, nice and neat, including my favorite, which was *My Fair Lady*.

Enjoying the Arnold's record collection was a treat I gave myself every single Thursday night after Ann was bathed and tucked in for the night. By the evening's end that one particular night, all the surfaces of my favorite albums were a mass of ripples.

My Fair Lady was also one of Mrs. Arnold's favorite albums.

Though I never got in trouble at the Arnold home, I had never (until then) melted their albums.

On the night of the "melting accident" Mr. Arnold came into the house to use the bathroom before driving me home. I was sitting on the sofa, having my usual end-of-the-night chat with Mrs. Arnold. Having those few minutes with her before going home was the highlight of my week; it was a little like how I felt when I sat with my mother years earlier, after school.

I wasn't aware, then, that the records had been ruined.

When Mr. Arnold moved past the stereo, and began climbing the steps a few at a time, he looked down. He stopped. His eyes landed on—then studied—the bunch of warped albums below.

"*Who* put these records on the hot receiver?" he yelled.

My eyes bugged out since I had never heard that tone from him before. I remember trying to think of an answer that wouldn't make things worse.

An answer that wouldn't get me fired.

Just then, Mrs. Arnold's voice sailed across the room, "Oh Norman, I think I must have done that earlier this evening!" Can you imagine? She was so convincing in her lie, that for a minute, even *I* thought she melted those records!

It was a perfect solution. Mr. Arnold thought Mrs. Arnold was a queen: to take her out to dinner was the joy of his life. So, for her to say *that*, meant that I was definitely not going to get in trouble!

Neither was she.

The point of the story is that I must have listened to those songs a hundred times before the night of the accident. So now, I know most of them by heart. And here we are— singing "Wouldn't It Be Loverly?" in the choir.

At rehearsal, like at the dances with Sofia, I forget that I have an angel as a friend.

At choir practice, I think instead, "It's exciting to hear my voice joined with everyone else's." Right then, I feel like dancing.

Anyway, Maura is one of the popular girls, and I only know her because at school, everyone gets to sit by someone according to the alphabetical order of their last names, even in the choir. She is Maura O'Hara and I'm Katie Neumann. There you go.

I went to Maura's house one day, between school letting out and the beginning of choir practice. We sat at the kitchen table: Maura, me, and Mrs. O'Hara.

I couldn't help noticing that their home is like a rich person's home: beautiful new furniture, lots of space, and all the countertops shiny. I couldn't find a chore to do if I tried.

A little earlier, as we came into the kitchen, I noticed that Maura was gliding around the kitchen like a ballerina, opening the refrigerator, taking out snacks—milk, cookies, and a banana. She was really happy and free, like I used to be in our kitchen on Cook Street, in my coal mining town.

Mrs. O'Hara looked at Maura, like she had waited all day for her to come home. Before we sat down, I saw Maura playfully kiss her mother's cheek. Then, like a firefly, glide past her mother, to make a landing on the chair nearest to her. Awed, I thought, "I forgot that mothers and daughters can be like this."

When we both sat at the kitchen table with our snacks, I was relieved that Maura lived close to the school. I didn't. I felt safe knowing that she probably would never come to my house. I was glad she wouldn't hear Eugenia screaming or see the laundry piled on every step for us to carry to the bedrooms.

My friend would never know that in my house, things were different—the way they looked, and the way you felt when you were there.

Mrs. O'Hara sat at the kitchen table with us. Maybe it was my imagination, but I think her eyes twinkled when she said, "Isn't my Maura beautiful?"

Really, if I were being completely honest, I would have to say that I hadn't thought about it before—whether Maura was beautiful or not.

If I *did* think about it, and if it wouldn't be rude, I would say, "In a way, her face reminds me of a horse."

Then I could add, "I *did* notice that Maura reminds me of a mischievous forest creature, which I think is an awesome thing to be."

What I managed to say was, "Oh yes!"

It's hard to figure out what to say when you have to think fast about things that are new. To answer questions without hurting people's feelings.

Then, as Mrs. O'Hara reached across the table, taking Maura's hand in hers, she looked first at her, then at me, and asked, "Isn't my Maura the smartest girl in the world?"

The two of them looked at each other as if they talked about that a lot, as if it was fun to say those things, as if they *believed* that I'd have fun agreeing. They didn't think that maybe I was embarrassed that Maura is in the "advanced" classes and I'm in the regular college prep classes (which in my opinion is a mistake).

How would *I* know, from sitting next to her in the choir, if she's smart or not?

"Yes, for sure," I said to Mrs. O'Hara, trying to sound believable.

When I think about it now, it's kind of creepy. Who does that? Aren't teenagers supposed to be irritated by so much sweet talk from their mothers? And aren't normal eleventh-grade girls supposed to be rolling their eyes to show that their mothers are ridiculous?

I admit, that my own father sometimes would ask my brothers' friends, "Isn't my Katie beautiful?" Sometimes he would say, "Isn't my Katie smart?" His eyes would twinkle, then he would pause, and stare at them to be sure *they* knew that he was talking about someone totally brilliant.

They always said, "Yes, Mr. Neumann."

But *I* didn't think it was great. I felt like he was trapping people or being weird. It's very different when your *father* says it, but I do give him credit for trying.

Maybe it was because of him that I secretly entered a beauty contest at Hess's Department Store, and they put a photograph of me wearing one of their new outfits in the window. I won a purse.

The Hess's contest was good evidence that I wasn't ugly, even if my brothers and sisters said it was a joke to think that I could win a beauty contest. (I hadn't counted on someone actually *seeing* my picture in Hess's window.)

I think, in our family, we were forgetting how to be nice to each other. Life wasn't what it used to be for any of us, and so many situations that made up our new life, ended up with all of us being angry— and sometimes mean— for no reason.

On that day after choir rehearsal, when I walked back home alone, I felt like I had stones in my stomach.

I wished that I had my own mother to ask Maura O'Hara, "Isn't *my* Katie beautiful?"

She would ask it in that tone of voice that says, "We all know it's obvious, but won't it be great to hear it out loud, so we can all enjoy it!"

She would say to Maura, "Isn't my Katie the smartest girl in the world?"

Because Maura would be a guest in *our* home, she would have to say, "Oh yes, for sure!"

As I was thinking that way, I had to brush tears from my eyes.

I passed some store windows on Hamilton Street and couldn't help turning to look at my reflection, to see who I was. What I saw was a girl hunched over, like her books were too heavy. I didn't recognize her.

All of this—the visit with Maura's mother, the choir rehearsal, the tears—occurred about six hours before my angel visited again.

Chapter 9

Tasting Pennies   1965

After my chores, I'm in my room "doing homework"—except, I'm not.

The way Maura's mother loves her returns to my mind like a movie scene caught in a loop. How she waits for Maura to come home. How she and Maura look at each other—enjoying every moment together. Tears start, but I don't know why.

Mrs. O'Hara isn't *my* mother. Why should I care? It isn't anyone's fault that *my* mother isn't in our kitchen after school. It would be perfect if I could find a way to not be sad, but that probably isn't going to happen.

Just thinking about it makes me tired. I give up on my homework altogether.

Before I reach my bed, I know … I'm not alone.

I take my place on the side of the bed and wait. It's not strange any more that I look toward the spot in the room, where I know my angel waits.

What looks like tiny, spinning pieces of gossamer begins to take the shape of my angel. It isn't even a small moment before we begin speaking, like old friends.

"I would like to talk about your mother," she says.

I'm *shocked* by this.

No one, and I do mean *no* one has said *that* to me.

Even *I* don't think it would be a good idea to talk *about* my mother. Maybe, I worry, I would start to cry in a whole new way and be swallowed—whole—by those tears.

"I don't think that would be a good idea," I say, thinking about the trillions of times when all I wished for was to have my mother talk to me (which, as you know, she never did).

But that was so very different from letting someone talk *about* her.

The angel waits.

I wait.

I'm thinking that my angel should come up with a better idea than talking about my mother, when I notice the taste of *pennies* in my mouth.

This is always a sign that the habit I've recently started has kicked up.

When I'm stressed out, I bite the inside of my mouth until it bleeds. I chew away the skin: first on one side, then the other, then back again. My mouth is swollen, hurting inside. Disgusting.

I'm tasting my own blood.

Mr. Gillmore, my science teacher says, "The copper in pennies tastes the same as a metal in blood."

It's not like I decide, "Oh, why don't I bite the inside of my mouth until it bleeds, until my mouth's swollen."

No, it's not planned like that. I just do it because, in a way, it seems to help me avoid thinking about my problems.

"I'm sorry that you've hurt your mouth," my angel said, reminding me that she seems to know an awful lot about what's going on with me.

"Sometimes it's very hard to do things, even when doing them might help," she says. For someone kind, she doesn't give up.

I know she's hoping I'll let her say things about my mother.

Still, I wait. It's the only thing I can manage to do.

As if she's made a decision, her voice changes. I'm not sure if she's giving in or trying to help me out.

She makes a suggestion, "Maybe you could just *think* about it for a while."

With that one sentence, she is gone.

And there I am, alone.

Relieved.

I notice that the inside of my mouth feels raw and sick. And that's OK, because right now, I feel like I'm very small inside, and that it hurts to be in the world.

Still, I know—as sure as day follows night—she's coming back.

Chapter 10

You Are Her Flower   1965

Mom, I wish you could talk to me. My angel still comes to my room. I know she's good, but the problem is—just when I start to trust her, stop feeling like a crazy girl for having her show up—

She starts saying, "We should talk about your mother."

She came to my room last night and made me so nervous that I bit my mouth inside. My mouth hurts like crazy.

Do you think I'm giving myself cancer?

I complain every time I talk to you. I'm sorry about that. If you're sick of hearing it, I don't blame you (you could skip the next ten lines of this letter and I'd never know)— I still wish you didn't die. Why can't I be a normal person? Everything keeps changing and nothing gets better.

Eugenia is meaner than ever. Daddy's having fights with her about her meanness, which he never wins. I hate my new school. Other people have mothers (which is a big problem—because I don't). Now, my angel is causing my mouth-biting problem to show up worse than ever.

I miss you a hundred times a day. When I'm not missing you, I'm biting myself. When too many rats are in cages they bite their tails and die. Mr. Gillmore again. It's as if, now, I'm the rat in the cage, biting myself.

I'm dying, Mommy, and if you don't do something ... who knows what'll happen

Not to threaten you or anything but if I die, the kids will be in trouble. You should think of Izzie and Andrew and Olivia Marie. They don't have one memory of you. Could you allow them to be alone with Eugenia forever? I know they'd still have Sofia, John Conner, and Evan. But we can't be sure that someday they wouldn't need only me.

My angel came three nights after having her bright idea—to talk about my mother. She acted like there wasn't a problem between us, like she thought we were both doing just fine.

Looking at her, I'm thinking, "Nothing seems to bother you." A small smile peaks from her mouth, as she looks at me.

She speaks quietly, softly, as if there's no situation whatsoever, "I wonder if you might allow me to say a few things?"

Though I'm a little worried, I'm feeling just a tiny bit braver then before.

Out comes a thought, timid as a mouse, "Yes..."

"I guess that would be ok."

And so, she begins.

"Your mother lives in you."

Silence.

She whispers, "You continue her."

Though I'm not sure I understand this, the idea seems OK ... for now.

"Look at your hands," my angel tells me.

Looking down I hear her ask, "What do you see?"

I look. And I look.

I know that I'm seeing the same hands that carry my books. These hands do the dishes. I'm used to them. I know them.

As if she hears these thoughts she says, "And what else do you see?"

Wondering if something might be impossible *and* real, at the same time—still looking down—I see my mother's hands.

I say, "They're mine *and* hers."

"Even my right index finger has a curved nail, just like my mother's. I never noticed that before."

Looking at my hands, I remember how *her* hands rubbed my belly when I was five and had a stomachache.

Looking at my hands I'm back in the kitchen on Cook Street. It's 1960 instead of 1964.

In this strange moment, I'm a Junior in high school in my bedroom, but also a 12-year-old girl watching wide-eyed as her mother skillfully removes the beater from the electric mixer. Its dripping cake batter is a tease.

I'm catching each precious drip. My tongue, my fingers, my head—dart under and over the beater. Part of the fun is that I'm now wearing a chocolate clown face, laughing because even the chocolate that lines my cheeks will find a path to my mouth.

Those beautiful hands bring me that beater, loaded with dripping cake mix, every Saturday for as long as I can remember. I stand inches away from her, knowing she'll give me this gift.

It's hard to know right now, standing with my angel, exactly what's happening. And yet, I can see myself licking that batter from the beater, its chocolaty sweetness as real as ever.

I see my mother's smiling face. My giggles are hers too. I like that we're a team. Both of us know that the whole family will have this cake tomorrow after Sunday dinner.

Looking at my hands, I REALLY see hers.

As I see, I remember how her hands put salve on my burnt hand on a day long ago, when Mrs. Zajac came to our kitchen for a cup of coffee.

The day when I couldn't rest until I ironed my first handkerchief, and—by mistake—burned my hand.

I felt such happiness that day and now. It doesn't matter that my hand (years later) seems to sting with a mild echo of pain. The happiness is there, because *my mother* rescued me from my hideout in the bathtub that day, and from my shame that I wouldn't listen to her when she tried to make me understand that I wasn't *quite* ready for ironing chores.

My angel said, "They are *your* hands, but because your mother lives in you, they're *her* hands too. When you bring someone a gift, your mother continues—in you. When you hold someone's hand or gently touch your sister or brother, *she* continues in you."

Then the angel says, "Just as your mother continues in your physical body, she continues in your heart, in your gestures, in your smile—in your imaginings."

I'm not biting my mouth now. Something inside me feels completely new. Completely true.

And then, as if the angel knows that I want more from her she says: "Your mother wants you to remember—that you are her flower, and she is your roots. A flower needs roots to survive. Without the roots the flower will die."

I'm not even thinking now. I'm just sitting there like a person who just saw the sky open and a miracle happen in a world where no one else saw anything like it before.

A thought came then, maybe from deep inside: "When a mother dies, maybe you don't lose *all* of her."

I'm starting to understand—as I look down at my own hands, seeing clearly now, that they're *her* hands.

I feel something as huge as the earth itself, opening inside me.

But my angel isn't finished.

"Your mother—all of us—want you to open your heart, to make space for *yourself*. She wants you to make space in your heart for others. She wants you to know that you're part of a precious community."

"What do you mean by … all of us?"

Before I can say something more, before I can ask something more.

My angel is gone.

If you were there, you'd see a girl staring at her hands— as if they were changed forever.

You'd be looking at a girl, no longer alone in the world, a girl whose mother was in some way, no longer the lady who fell off a cliff—leaving her daughter alone.

It's true, that the lonely, and even the abandoned feelings would return from time to time, but the angel's message seemed to diminish the *power* of those feelings.

If you were there, you'd see a girl who walked a little taller and smiled a little bit more.

Chapter 11

Mother Knows Best   1958

When you're a kid like me, you spend a lot of time thinking about small things that happened before everything turned upside down. Things that you used to take for granted because they were part of *normal* life. You'd be having one of those memories, then two seconds later—it's *happening* in your mind. You're telling yourself the story—completely forgetting that your mother died. But when you remember, and you always do, it's like having a boulder fall on your heart.

Right now is an excellent time to tell one of those memories—for two reasons.

First, when my angel had me looking at my hands the other night, I remembered getting burned in 1958 like it was yesterday. My mother's tenderness that day came, too.

Second, after my angel's last visit—when memories come—I have a completely different feeling. I'll tell the whole story first then, I'll explain how the *afterwards* part is different.

73

"Mom, can I iron this handkerchief?"

Mrs. Zajac and my mom are deep into some juicy story. Their eyes focus like lasers on each other, each finishing the other's sentences. I figure that this is a good time to *pretend* that it's normal, for me, a ten-year-old, to iron a handkerchief.

Maybe my mother won't remember that I haven't ironed anything in my entire life.

Mom and Mrs. Zajac are happy, like I would be at Tagananni's Pizza Parlor, shaking a bottle of fresh oregano on the deliciously greasy, melted cheese—drooling at the idea of my first bite.

This wonderful treat wouldn't be pierogi, or potato pancakes, or even chocolate cake.

This would be pizza pie!

Mrs. Zajac's visits in our kitchen, especially this day when my mother had been ironing, make me hope that my mother will be distracted enough to allow me to have a personal adventure.

"Mom, PLEASE! Can I do some ironing? I'll be careful. I'm ten. That's old enough to iron."

"No." My mother looks me straight in the eye. "You'll get to iron soon enough," as she turns to Mrs. Zajac to finish her story. They both touch the cups of Maxwell House coffee in front of them—like they're precious possessions.

Both women are free for ten minutes from their mother-duties. Between them they have seven children—children who are always running around; wanting attention, or water, or diapers changed; or nagging them for treats. But on this day, in this short pile of minutes, it's just the three of us in that kitchen.

"I PROMISE I'll be careful. I'll go slow. I'll *watch* what I'm doing."

My strategy—as I stand next to the abandoned ironing board— is to wear her down.

"Mommeee," I say like I'm a three-year-old. Please! Please! Please!"

This nagging is a fine art, perfected by children all over the world.

Hardly looking at me, my mother says the magic words, "Just one small piece."

We, (the ironing board, the iron and I), are only two feet to her right. She's right there if I have a question. She's "watching out" for me.

I'm dying from happiness as I place a handkerchief on the ironing board. It's wet, rolled up tight, until I flatten it. Slowly. Carefully.

I've seen my mother do this so many times before.

I position the hot, heavy iron on a small corner of the material, and start to glide the iron from one corner to the next.

"This is so easy, so great. I'm just like my mother," I remember thinking.

I look at my mother, wanting to share this moment, to hear my mother say, "My Katie is *so* smart."

"My Katie can do anything."

"My Katie—"

They're still deep in conversation, mom and Mrs. Zajac—laughing, putting their heads close together—as if their secret story is getting to a really wonderful part. I don't even care, because my grown-up moment fills me like a puff fish.

It's then that confusion, pain and shock all tumble through me at once.

Looking down, I see my hand on the ironing board— sandwiched between a small sad handkerchief and a heavy, hot iron!

I realize that in the nanosecond it took for me to look toward my mother—the iron had moved, as if on a mission to reach the other end of the handkerchief, not caring that my hand was in the way.

Is it possible that, as I looked at my mother, the motion of the iron over the handkerchief *continued*. That I had forgotten to stop moving the iron? Even as it ran across my hand?

My first thought is "Oh no, she'll be mad." It doesn't matter that she never is. Well only one time, when I gave her an extremely "dirty" look—a disrespectful look.

Somehow, I confuse the flash of pain with that thought, "She'll be so mad."

I quickly and quietly stand the iron up on its end.

Quieter still, I walk slowly, almost on tiptoe, out of the kitchen.

The pain inside my hand is like a white-hot knife, throbbing ugly and deep. Worse than stomach cramps. Worse than a bee sting. Much worse than anything I've ever known. It's so foreign a pain that I can't even look at my hand.

By some dumb logic, I decide on a good course of action: Go up the stairs, through the hall, and sit in the empty bathtub. Pull the shower curtain closed (for privacy). Rock back and forth. Hold my hand close to my chest. Rock some more. Moan (quietly).

I think, "Yes, this will help."

Minutes pass.

The pain increases until I want to sink like a rock into nothingness.

It's then that I hear my mother's voice, "Where's my Katie?" It's a kind voice, a loving voice, and concerned.

And yet I think, "Oh no, I'm in trouble."

As she pulls back the shower curtain, I look up, ashamed, so disappointed in my failure to be a good ironer.

Relief washes over me as she helps me up, almost singing something that feels like, "There. There."

That thing a mother says to a little baby who's crying. But I don't mind because my burnt hand makes me feel very small.

If you were me in that bathroom, you'd feel that you had a very good mother: one who only makes things better. One who never mentions that she tried to tell you that you were too young to iron a handkerchief.

You'd be relieved that your mother doesn't say her standard line with you, which is, "You have ants in your pants," which translates, "You can't sit still for two minutes without getting into trouble."

You'd have had a mother who doesn't mind that her visit with her friend is over.

As she reaches for some cream, and softly dabs it on your hand, you could finally look at it. That it's covered with angry blisters is OK.

Because you, AND your mother, are looking at it together.

If you were me, you wouldn't know if it was the cream that made the pain different, and smaller, or her presence, in that tiny bathroom.

You wouldn't forget how much you love her if you lived to be fifty.

If you were me in 1964, before the angel's visits, having the old story going on in your head, you'd be feeling OK.

You'd be thinking, "Wow. It's great to love your mother so much, and great to know that if you burn yourself, she'll be nice to you."

But, about two seconds later, the sadness would come back, like a nightmare you can't do anything about.

Before your angel started helping you, you'd *have to remember*, "I'm a girl whose mother died. No matter what I say or do, nothing will change that." The hurt inside, would be about the same as if someone burned you, all over, with a hot iron.

But something is *changing*.

Since the night when my angel helped me see my hands—my mother's hands—my mother's no longer *completely* gone ... not *completely* disappeared forever.

The change is: I have *proof*. Just by looking down at my own hands—I can *know*—the memories we had together help my mother *live* inside me, even if it's in a way I can barely imagine.

The whole thing is like a good mystery.

This help I'm getting from my angel is coming just in the nick of time, because I'm starting to have a very different kind of trouble in my life. It's about the kids I'm spending time with in the evenings—during the summer.

Mostly, it's about Eugenia. She has absolutely NO idea about the Number One Rule for being a good mother: If you think you're a mother (or a step-mother), kindness is as important as breathing.

My biggest problem is that I'm starting to have some mean and dangerous thoughts about Eugenia. Some situations end up with me being *very* angry.

If you were me—and loved telling and hearing stories, as much as I do (which I definitely do)—you might want to give each part of "the Eugenia problem" its own name. That's exactly what I decided to do.

So I named them,

Hanging Out

Trapped Insect, and

Saying Bad Things

Chapter 12

Hanging Out   1965

"Eric Logan's here," John Conner screams up the steps toward my bedroom. With that announcement, a loud burp tumbles out of my brother's mouth. His boring attempt to embarrass me.

"Mission accomplished," I yell down the steps.

I continue to get ready for my date, wishing I belonged to a different family. If my brothers acted like *Leave It to Beaver's* Wally Cleaver, that would work. At least a person could count on Wally for some manners.

Eric and I are both in the 11th grade. Our "dates" consist of walking around the block one or two times, holding hands, and having a three-sentence conversation. Tops.

The walks end at Kramer's drugstore, which my father can see from the front porch. I make a point to never look at the porch to avoid having to wave hello if my father happens to be standing on the porch, looking my way.

No one says very much at "the corner." They just nod at the kids who come and stand there and ignore anyone who goes inside. It's cool to not say very much, as if everyone's too mature to need to make small talk. Hanging out there on summer nights makes me feel normal.

Part of the routine at the drugstore is that Buddy Denko and Marie Lehman have fights. They're both in 11th grade at Allen High, but seem older, maybe because they're so serious all the time. No one else joins in their arguments, or even knows what's going on. The fights happen in angry whispers. Buddy and Marie sort of walk down the street as soon as their voices get tense, which is almost immediately.

The rest of us start to feel more comfortable then, because to us, the fights are boring like a song that's irritating when it doesn't tell a good story. If I'm being completely honest, I have to admit that the boring part isn't one hundred percent true for me.

There's something important between the both of them and it makes me curious. They seem close, as if they're in love, even if they're not very happy. I study how they look when the fight starts, trying to figure them out. Marie's very short, as pretty as anyone I've ever seen, maybe a little bit pudgy, and usually upset.

You wouldn't call Buddy skinny, which makes him a good fit for Marie. But that's beside the point. I wonder if he's just a regular jerk like a lot of boys. Not able to keep from doing dumb things.

Marie's head is usually bent low. What you can see of her mouth is that it's constantly pouting. Buddy seems clueless. I give him credit for trying to fix the thing that's causing the trouble.

Eric and I like to pass the time together. We never fight over anything. The most important thing about us, is that I feel kind of safe with him. He's sweet and gets melty around me, which I like. But that's a different way of being boy-friend-and-girlfriend.

Different from Buddy and Marie.

When I think about the whole thing—the difference between Eric and me, and Buddy and Marie—it's as if it's a good puzzle that doesn't really need to be solved. Interesting to wonder about.

An agreement between Mr. Kramer and all of us who hang out at his drugstore has two parts:

His first rule, "You kids need to be quiet."

And the second, which he doesn't need to repeat, "The *first* time any of my customers complains about you kids—it'll be the last."

Since the rules are basically easy to follow, everyone seems to be happy enough (with the exception of the mysterious arguing between Buddy and Marie).

One day in late October, two months after those summer dates with Eric, I'm returning from school to get a completely unexpected shock from Eugenia.

Just minutes before I reach for the doorknob, my thoughts aren't about anything special. I'm still feeling a kind of happiness from enjoying the comforting rhythm of walking home from school. On these walks home, nothing is expected of me. I'm not worried about not having done my homework, or what to say to the girls at the lunch table.

On these walks home, I just get to be me.

I'm happy too, because the one exception to school boredom is English class. We're studying the myth of *Demeter and Persephone*. I like it so much that it doesn't matter that I'm not in the advanced classes. I'm the only one who actually likes the story. It doesn't seem to be a problem with the other kids that I answer most of Mrs. Anderson's questions. (Maybe they think that *my* taking up so much class time gets *them* off the hook.) What happened today is a good example:

"Can anyone summarize the myth we're currently studying?" Mrs. Anderson asks.

I don't miss a beat, saying, "Hades the god of the under-world— the god who lives under the sea, kidnaps Demeter's daughter Persephone while she's picking flowers by a stream."

In the quiet of the room, I say, "Demeter, the goddess of the earth, can't stop crying or searching for her daughter. Whether the people like it or not, *everyone* has to suffer because of it—"

"Absolutely," says Mrs. Anderson, "Can you remember why?"

"Demeter's not only a mother to Persephone, she's the goddess of the earth, so her grief causes the earth to die, and famine happens everywhere because she's too sad to do her goddess job."

I go on, "When someone's daughter is kidnapped, life shouldn't be normal for everyone else, as if *no one's* child is missing, as if *no one* is suffering—"

"You have a strong opinion—" Mrs. Anderson's voice sounds tentative.

I ignore an inner confusion at her comment, thinking that most people would see the situation the way I do. Not knowing what else to say, I go on. "Because so many people are suffering, an oracle decides to help Demeter get her daughter back for six months out of every year."

"Does anyone know why myths matter, even thousands of years later?" she asks.

I raise my hand. But the bell rings, saving everyone from my sure-to-be-too-long answer.

I understand completely that you're not supposed to take myths literally.

I'm remembering Mrs. Anderson's words from yesterday, "The real value of myths is that they help our lives *cohere*—"

I *loved* that she used that word.

I think, maybe there's an invisible *thread* that runs through our lives that sort of connects everything together in a way we can't see.

It makes me wonder, if understanding that connection means that we become solid— *we cohere*— we're connected to our personal past, and also to a mystery. We're *bigger than our own story!* Sometimes, when I think about that, I feel a little confused, and also hopeful. Excited even.

When Mrs. Anderson said that myths help us cohere, I heard Paul Shaughnessy let out a disgusting yawn, which reminds me of the boys-being-jerks problem.

At Central Catholic, no one thought you were a weirdo if you liked mythology as long as you didn't try to talk about it at the lunch table.

One of the rules was that the lunch table was a place for giggling, and boy talk. It was there that I listened in astonishment at the way the other girls joked about their behavior with boys, about the way they enjoyed—or made fun of—almost everything concerning that alien species.

Anita Searfoss had the most unusual mouth. It was special, like someone thought to draw her mouth in the shape of a ready-to-get-kissed pucker. She had popped-out round eyes, making her look like she had just been pinched. They moved in a fun way when she told stories.

Anita's eyes looked at you like, "I'm s-o-o-o entertained."

Last night I tried to make my own mouth and eyes look like hers in front of the mirror in the bathroom. I looked like there was something wrong with me, so I gave it up.

Earlier today, Anita's eyes were dancing when she said, "I pinned my bra shut with a safety pin in the back, right before Andrew picked me up for the dance."

All eyes shifted to me for a reaction. They knew I probably wouldn't *get* the joke, which I mostly never did when it came to boy talk. To them, my confused reactions were part of the fun. Since they weren't mean—at least, *mostly* not mean—I didn't mind. Instead, I focused my energy on trying to tamp down my cluelessness.

Anita hesitated, like someone who offers a piece of candy, then pulls it away when you reach for it.

Joanie Cooney asked, "Are you going to tell us what happened next, or not?"

I wondered if she knew she was leaning so far across the table that her sweater fell into a load of ketchup.

"We-l-l," Anita said, "the dance was boring, but then ... we went to Cedar Park."

All of us knew she was talking about the necking hangout. She had everyone's attention—even mine.

"Andrew's saying, 'You're so beautiful. You're sooooooo beautiful.' In two minutes, his hands are all over me and he's reaching for the back of my bra!"

The girls giggled. Her stories oozed juiciness. I did all I could to muster a fake smile. I'm the baby of the group who hasn't ever gone to Cedar Park. I didn't see the humor (which, I knew, made me uncool).

As if she was back at Cedar Park reliving the story, Anita continued, "He's kissing me like crazy. His hands start *undoing* my bra like he's Mr. Man. He's working and working, but nothing happens, but he has to pretend that there's no problem."

Here, she paused for a few seconds, while the suspense tortured us all, even me.

"Well?" Carol Johnson egged her on, her hand groping for a potato chip.

From Anita, "He can't get the thing opened!"

By now the girls couldn't contain their laughter. I was embarrassed, stuck and uncomfortable at the part where,

"... his hands start undoing my bra."

The girls were having fun with Andrew's confusion *and* my embarrassment, which snuck onto my face (A-W-K-W-A-R-D).

If you've ever been uncomfortable but also happy to belong, you'll know what it felt like then, for me. I was relieved, in a way, that here at Central Catholic, sitting with the non-advanced class girls, no one knew that my mother died, or any details about me. I was learning, second hand, a little bit about boys and what fun looked like, at least for them. I was even learning, in a small way, how to be an 11th grade girl.

For instance, yesterday at the lunch table, Ann Arnold announced, "I'm applying to West Chester State."

Just like that, right then, I said to myself, "I'm going to do that, too."

The school counselor had mentioned to me that if I was going to college, I should apply to three schools. That was all she said. But after what Ann announced at the lunch table, I knew that I would apply to only West Chester State. I had a plan.

I'd borrow the fifty-dollar application fee from Sofia. (The fifty-dollar-per-application part of applying was why I'd have to settle for one school to try to get into). You probably remember that before my mother died, we were more or less a rich family. Since Eugenia showed up, that isn't true anymore. In my new life, everything seems to be about how much it costs "to feed seven children."

You wouldn't have to be a genius to figure out that Eugenia had a stingy attitude about money. Nothing was really different with my dad's job.

What this all meant for me, was that next to the other kids at Central Catholic, I was a poor kid. Because I had no intention of having them find out, I wouldn't mention borrowing the money from my sister.

All of those things (girl talk, boys, bras, West Chester State) moved through the back of my mind on that October day like the hum of a car you hardly notice.

If you're wondering why I was talking a little while ago about ugly, dangerous parts of me, well just be patient. Those parts are there, but they don't come out unless I *really* get pushed around.

Chapter 13

Trapped Insect   1965

Eugenia was at the front door, like a snake behind a rock.

"How *could* you spend every summer night at the corner with Marie Lehman *knowing* that she's a bad girl—with a *bad* reputation?The way Eugenia cackled the word *bad* reminded me of a witch, stirring a poison cauldron.

I was inside my house now, backed into the closed door. Not knowing what to say.

I didn't understand what Marie Lehman *did* that made her a bad girl. I didn't know why her being bad would make *me* bad. My confused silence made the situation worse.

Eugenia was leaning in now, with a small drip of spit sneaking from the side of her mouth. "*How* can you shame your family like this?"

I wanted to say something—anything—but I couldn't think of something that would please her. My mouth opened and closed, once, then again ...

Nothing came out.

That was when my second problem appeared.

I just finished reading *The Catcher in the Rye*. The main character, Holden Caulfield, has this favorite line: "He's a royal pain in the ass."

Whenever I read those words, or just thought about them—imagining them coming out of Holden's mouth—I started laughing. I couldn't stop. It was pretty much the ONLY thing in my life that I thought was funny!

"He's a royal pain in the ass." I would laugh at school in the middle of class.

"He's a royal pain in the ass." I would laugh by myself, sitting in my room at night.

Now, the worst words that could come to me, in my desperation to say *something* to Eugenia would be, "You're a royal pain in the ass."

Those words were right there, smack in the middle of my being struck dumb—in the middle of my being screamed at by Eugenia—for who knew what ...

Those words waved in my head like a red cape to a bull.

I silently *begged* myself, "No, *don't* let *that* come out."

I never tried anything harder than stopping those words.

And I *did* stop them. But—

I started to laugh.

As fast as the laughter came out—it stopped!

There it was: a flash of disrespect.

It seemed to me, that in those few seconds, she, a large woman, seemed to become even larger. The hallway was small on either side of us. I was jammed in tight against the door, with nowhere to go.

I was a trapped insect.

Apparently, Eugenia had some self-control of her own, because she didn't go down the "disrespect" road.

Instead, she stuck, like a bulldog to a bone, to her original mission: catching me at being bad. I was relieved, but exhausted with fear at what might have happened. Disrespecting adults was a huge offense in our "new" family. To be honest, it was a huge offense in our "old" family. The difference was that in our other family with our real mother, people usually weren't pains in the ass.

Eugenia marched on, "You're a sneak. You think I'm a fool? You think I don't know what's going on there?" Was she talking about all of us, months ago, hanging around the drugstore?

From me, more silence.

The look on Eugenia's red face started to look scary. Her anger, growing fast, reminded me of a balloon before it explodes with a pop!

It was in this moment, that the answer to a mystery came to me.

All the arguments between Marie and Buddy months before were because Marie was pregnant! Marie and Buddy were trying to figure out what to do.

It made sense to me that when Marie went away to "visit her aunt" then came back at the start of the school term it was about her having a baby!

Now, in October, she was back on 14th Street, and at Allan High finishing her 11th grade year.

At least one of my crimes, according to Eugenia, was that I "played her for a fool."

For one small second, I thought I could make things better with a harmless joke.

I could say, "He... he... that sounds like something Shylock would say in *The Merchant of Venice*."

I knew right away that "No, don't say that," was good advice to give myself. What's wrong with me? I'm losing it, I thought.

Eugenia seemed to think that I was somehow part of what she called "very loose and shocking sexual behavior." This included Marie's pregnancy, the gossip "that's all over the neighborhood," and a baby that Marie may have given away so that she would be allowed back in school. Eugenia's anger came down to *me* having "bad companions."

Finally, a pathetic response came out of my mouth: "I didn't know. Marie never said anything about a baby—to any of us."

Eugenia answered with something about "birds of a feather flocking together," and the whole family being dragged into this ugly story because of me.

I didn't know how to explain it, all I did was stand in front of Mr. Kramer's drugstore for a couple of months—with Eric Logan, Marie Lehman, and the other kids last summer.

I figured out a few days later, that Marie probably switched her white Oxford blouse (which she never tucked in) to a bigger size later in the summer. If that happened, how *would* I know?

I *do* know that "out-of-wedlock" pregnancies are not talked about.

No pregnant girls go to school because, as every adult seems to say," who knows *what* they might start. What message would *that* send to the other girls?"

No one *explained* that to me—not *exactly* in those words. I *have* noticed that girls who get pregnant *do* stop showing up at school until they aren't pregnant anymore.

"Well," from Eugenia, "I'll ask again. How could you do this to your family?"

"I ... "

"I *didn't* know."

I was still trying hard to make sense out of all that had happened with Marie, who was my friend, but only sort of—

We shared nods (a kind of hello) that summer, never stories, or problems, or phone calls. No girl talk like at the lunch table at Central Catholic. No one—least of all Eugenia—guessed that I was someone who had stopped being normal three years ago. I no longer had *close* girlfriends who shared real secrets. I *did* read books, tons of books, but that doesn't count.

My social life that summer consisted of conversations with Eric, and standing around with the kids at the drugstore.

No one knew why Eric and I kept "dating." Even *we* didn't know. It turned out he was shy and immature like me.

No one dreamed that neither one of us ever suggested a first kiss. We were more like 13-year-olds than 16-year-olds in that way. A few weeks ago, we broke up with no more fanfare than if we finished reading a good book.

And still, here was Eugenia, demanding, "How could you *not* know. She was seven or eight months pregnant!"

"She wore a white blouse every night that she never tucked in," I said.

That came out so weak that even I thought I was lying.

The problem for me, was a thought I kept to myself.

"I'm not sure why *I'm* bad, why *I'm* in trouble because Marie and Buddy had a baby." I kept that to myself so I could get out of that hallway. Away from Eugenia.

For the past three years, I haven't understood *anything*.

And worse.

I've started to have a crazy feeling that we should get rid of Eugenia, that having her in our lives is worse than our mother being dead.

The one good thing during the whole out-of-wedlock-bad-companions confusion was that, that night, my angel decided that we should have a talk.

Chapter 14

Saying Bad Things   1965

I wasn't surprised that my angel visited almost as soon as I turned out the lights. As so often happens, I couldn't see my angel at first, but still, she was there.

Just being together without speaking took up most of our time. I could see her now, from the corner of my eye, sitting, but not touching me, content to be at the foot of my bed. I didn't need to talk. She didn't talk either, at first.

Our being there, a team, reminded me of past days. I would come home from school to find my mother in her favorite chair, fingers barely moving across her rosary beads.

I—like a rabbit sitting quietly at the edge of the woods—would sit on the floor beside her. We didn't talk then, either. Being together had a special calm, a soft way of knowing that we weren't exactly two separate people.

Being quiet with my angel, I'm able to remember my mother's way of knowing everything important to me. Everything important *about* me. I was much younger then, and I didn't completely understand how my mother knew so much, or how she loved *all* of me. Her love freed me to just be me.

She allowed the confident part of me to open to the whole world, and to know that people were as good and kind as I needed them to be.

Or, if they weren't—if they were prickly or dismissive or hurtful—I could tell my mother. She would have a conversation with them, a conversation that would change them, or at least, change *my* way of seeing the situation.

One time, my mother worked her magic when I told her that Sister Anita never called on me in the third grade. My mother, hearing my disappointment and my feelings of upset (she liked to say, "feelings of upset" instead of anger), decided to have a talk with Sister Anita.

Sister Anita told my mother, it was "important to give others a chance at speaking in class, a chance to shine like Katie." My mother got me to realize that Sister Anita *did* call on me, but not every time. That was a little different than "never." She also made the "shining like Katie" matter more to me than feeling upset.

When my mother was with me, I could know that people would be nice. That I was good.

It was then, when I was thinking about my mother (able to let thoughts of her motherness sink in) that my angel spoke, "What you're feeling Katie, is what we call grace."

I looked over at her.

"Your way of being with her *now* is a reminder that you didn't lose *all* of your mother when she died that day."

"I really hate it when someone, even you, tries to tell me that it'll be okay. That it's not horrible that my mother isn't with any of us anymore. So, if that's what you're up to, you can save your breath."

"I saw what happened today, with Eugenia."

"Yeah... How could you miss it? I don't really care if you think I'm bad like she does, but I hate her so much that if I had a knife, I'd stab her in the throat."

"You would stab her with a knife?"

"In her throat," I said.

Seeing me glance at her with *fear*, as if my words *and* my ugly heart would surely chase an angel back to heaven forever, the angel spoke.

"And when you say that you could have stabbed her, what do you feel—deep down?"

"What would anyone feel if they said that?"

"You're you. So anyone else doesn't really matter right now. Does it?"

Silence seemed to fill the room now. This is what the angel does when she's being stubborn. She waits, as if there's no hurry.

"What do *I* feel when I say, 'I'd stab her with a knife?'"

"That was the question."

Again, I sat there, thinking.

A wild feeling came up from my stomach, and went right to my throat, which really hurt—like on the day of my mother's funeral. But I sat there anyway, with that feeling in my body, and in my heart.

Then, I heard myself crying. I felt my angel's hand on mine.

I cried until my face was wet and my nose was leaking, and saliva was drooling out of my mouth.

When my tears were winding down, something happened inside. I noticed that my anger had changed.

We sat together a few minutes more. "You're feeling sadness now," my angel said. "It's a truer feeling, child, truer than rage. What's happening now, inside?"

"I'm tired. It's a good tired."

"Is there peace?"

I'm thinking that maybe it is peace. As if she knows this she speaks again.

"That's also a grace to you. Because you're perfect, and beautiful, peace is ... is *meant* to follow tears."

"Even when I say bad things?"

"Even then."

Her voice has a way of smiling, of saying by its very sound, "You are mine, child. You need to know that with the problem at the drugstore—with your friend Marie—you did nothing wrong."

Moving closer, as if to whisper, she said, "Sometimes Eugenia is hurtful. Maybe she just needs time to become a more skillful mother."

"I don't like it when people defend her. I get angry at that. Her friends and my father's, they say she's an angel for 'stepping in to be our mother.'"

"And that makes you angry?"

"Yes, because my mother would never treat us the way she does. If my mother could see how she acts when my father's not around, she would take a knife and—"

"And what?"

I didn't say anything because my mother wouldn't take a knife to anyone. My angel knows that, and so do I.

Finally, I said, "She would tell her to leave. To not come back. She would say, "These are *my* children."

Smiling ever so slightly, I said, "At least *you're* here."

"Yes."

She added, "You might find your own way to speak to Eugenia someday—to say your truth with a gentle heart."

Just when I thought she'd leave like she usually did—as quickly and quietly as she came—she asked a question.

"Is it even a tiny bit possible, that you would like Eugenia to love you? That at least, you need her to be kind to you?"

"No, I hate her. She is ugly, fat, stupid, *and* mean to my brothers and sisters."

"Well, I guess you answered *that* question."

As we sat for a few minutes, I heard a big sigh creep out of me.

And then she said, "There's just one thing I'd like you to think about. You don't even need to respond, not now anyway—

"Maybe you could just let the idea … rattle around quietly for a few days, or even a few months—or years."

"OK," I said, trying to hide my speck of curiosity.

"I wonder if Eugenia's being in your life, in the lives of your brothers and sisters—harsh and unskillful as she is—means that no one will take Izzie away from you. No one will think that a man with seven young children can't possibly take care of six children *and* an infant all by himself."

"Is it possible," she continued, "that because of Eugenia's presence in your family, Izzie won't, in the end, be raised by those people in Ashley—the ones that had expressed a desire to raise her?"

I was stunned. I never told my angel about those polite, but strange-acting people who had offered to adopt Izzie after my mother died. I never told *anybody*. How could she know that I worried about that?

There wasn't anything really *wrong* with the Gabla family, but I knew they weren't the kind of people who would let their children have Elvis blasting while they did the dishes, while they danced with the refrigerator handle to rock and roll. Or have water fights, even if the floor got all wet. I couldn't bear to think of Izzie missing life with all of us. No, the Gabla's weren't really strange. They suffered from properness.

It was that fear of being separated before Dad married Eugenia, that made me give the kids baths, even when they didn't need them. I took lots of pictures: clean and shiny kids, saying the Rosary next to a big picture of their mother. This would be evidence that we didn't *need* anyone to take Izzie from us. Those pictures were my insurance.

Was it possible that my angel heard the gossip I heard—that Mrs. Yatko whispered one day, to my grandma, over the fence, that maybe letting the Gabla's adopt Izzie would be best for everyone?

As I start to respond, my angel softly raised a finger to her mouth. With that gesture, her eyes looked at me like I was *really* perfect in every way.

And then she was gone.

If you were there, you'd notice that I wasn't quite so angry after that. Mean thoughts weren't coming out (so much) either. Still, I wouldn't be telling the truth if I pretended that our new life with Eugenia was working out, or that I started liking her.

Once in a while, I did give some thought to the question my angel asked about all of us being able to stay together because of Eugenia.

But I couldn't really find a good answer.

Chapter 15

Family Meeting   1965

If you were me, you wouldn't be too surprised to hear your father and Eugenia yelling in the basement. There seemed to be more fights every day.

Somehow "the kids" were always the reason for the problems. Either John Conner forgot to take out the garbage, or Dad would yell, "They're *my kids* and I need to spend some time with *them too!*"

Eugenia complained, "I'd like some time with you, John!" (She had more time with my father than my mother *and* my grandmother ever had, combined.)

It wasn't long after she came to live with us that we had a "family meeting" (the first and last).

Three things happened at that meeting:

One: I said *two* things. One was a question. One was a little comment.

Two: Eugenia ran upstairs and came down with a suitcase in her hand.

Three: She left.

That was the whole family meeting.

As she slammed the front door, she said (about me), "I don't need to take *that* from a sixteen-year-old." And out she goes.

What I said wasn't really that bad.

At the meeting, *none* of us wanted to talk, even though we knew Daddy wanted us to say what was bothering us.

We older kids understood what Daddy didn't: Eugenia wouldn't like our talking at all. We figured it out because she managed to do most of her mean things when Daddy was working.

None of us wanted to make more problems. We didn't want to start more fighting by complaining.

I wanted to say, "Daddy, a family meeting probably wouldn't work. If Mommy was alive, it would. But not now." I couldn't say it now with *all* of us sitting there.

Daddy wouldn't let it go. The parlor was full of all seven of us kids, Eugenia, and Daddy, all staring at each other.

Daddy kept saying, "Well, we're here to try to become a better family. Somebody needs to say what's on their mind."

Part of me wanted to help him out, but I couldn't stand nasty, sneaky Eugenia, who happened to be the problem, so I thought, "Don't say *anything*."

Silence can last a long time. It can make you *have to* say something.

After about ten minutes, and not being able to endure the silence, I looked straight at Eugenia and said, "You don't love us."

She sat up straight, with that know-it-all look on her face.

"You're not my blood," she said like that was supposed to explain everything. It would, if the person saying it were a monster.

She said it, *in front of* my father! That gave me courage to say what *I* thought about that—OUT IT CAME:

"Someday, you'll be old and alone and *nobody* will love you."

I guess, in a way, I said that, about her not loving us to trap her—to make her show her meanness in front of Daddy. And it worked. When she slammed the door that day, suitcase in hand, all of a sudden it was as if a bright sun came out.

"I thought, "Eugenia's a royal pain in the ass."

The problem was, Daddy looked like somebody beat him up. His face looked frightened—like it did in the months after my mother died. He grabbed his keys and ran after her.

"I'll be right back." That's all he said. He got into his own car and drove off.

Though he called to say he was thinking about us, he didn't come home for three days. It was weird to be alone for so long with the little kids, but pretty nice to have Eugenia gone. When he did come home, she was with him.

I figured out that he spent those days talking her into coming back.

I knew we wouldn't have any more family meetings.

A week later, the whole house is quiet as a church, but not *peaceful* like a church. It feels like everybody's nervous, mad, or scared. Then, like a flashfire, the house is full of screaming and cursing.

From my father, "I don't give a damn. This is my house and I've made up my mind."

From Eugenia, muffled protests, but I can't make out words.

My father again, "Are you saying that my sister is interfering? Anyone can see that she's giving us a gift here." That's when I remembered that Aunt Terry called the house the night before.

He must mean that she is *not* interfering.

Eugenia's arguing back, but I can't make out anything she says.

Dad spits back, "My children are not slaves for ****** ****!" (I can't hear the whole thing). I get the feeling, he's sticking up for us—for somebody.

I'm hoping he's telling her, "You need to do more of the adult chores."

(She *is* lazy).

I creep close to the cellar door, hoping that I can figure out what's going on. When the basement door flies open— I'm almost blasted from the kitchen.

Eugenia comes into the kitchen, looking straight at *me*, like I'm a huge monster. "*You're* going to your Aunt Terry's. Get yourself packed. Now!"

One day later, I'm saying goodbye to my dad, my brothers and sisters, and starting a vacation that would last from the middle of August to the day before school starts. I love my Aunt Terry and Uncle Nigel and had visited them before my mother died. Their two children, my cousins Gibby and Greg, are in elementary school.

Uncle Nigel only talks when he's teasing you. He pretends to be crabby, but he's funny. I can tell that he's happy that I'm there with his family. Not because I'll babysit, which I'm never asked to do, but because I belong there.

So for the next couple of weeks, I have fun being a teenager.

Aunt Terry takes me to jazz concerts in the park. I notice that her feet tap with the music.

The tension that lives in my house—like goop that seeps through the crack of every cupboard and door—isn't here at Aunt Terry and Uncle Nigel's. Aunt Terry talks like she's having a blast (with the news, or the story, or the latest secret).

Best of all, she and Uncle Nigel do *all* the work.

I get to hang out with them while they do it—hearing stories and being entertained. My two cousins hang around with us, too. They're curious. Their eyes twinkle like they just found a surprise—like they're about to share it.

I love my father for making this vacation happen. I don't even care *how* it happened, or that I didn't have time to say goodbye to my friends at the drugstore. For all I know, Mrs. Arnold didn't know I was gone until I didn't show up for babysitting on Thursday. I can't remember if I called her.

Everything happened like …

Boom! You're home.

Then …

Boom! You're not!

On the second day of my visit, Aunt Terry and I are taking a walk up the street. She's telling me about how her family didn't like my mother at first, because she was Polish. Then, they got to know her and they all loved her.

Mom invited them (Aunt Terry, Uncle Patrick, Uncle Paula *and* Grandma Aelish) for dinner every Sunday.

Aunt Terry says, "Your mother was a great baker. We all loved that she played poker with us in the evening."

Like it was surprising to her, she says, "It turned out— your mother was the best person ever."

"Duh… of course," I'm thinking as we walk.

If Aunt Terry's surprise at my mother's wonderfulness doesn't make sense to you, you need to know that I feel bad for Aunt Terry and my father, and all their brothers and sisters.

They had to grow up with Grandma's saying bad things about people for no reason. Then they'd be surprised when they found out that Grandma was wrong. I bet they heard Grandma say, a thousand times, about how no one should marry a Polack. I know this for a fact—I heard it, too!

If you don't believe me about the Polish thing, then you need to hear this:

One day, my grandma's walking down the street with my sister Olivia Marie. Grandma's complaining about Paula (one of her daughters-in-law). When she goes on about people, you have to be very quiet, or she'll turn her attention to you—about being lazy, or stupid, or generally terrible.

Grandma says, (about Aunt Paula) like it's a normal thing to say, "That Polish bitch looks like a skunk, with that gray stripe crawling up her head."

Aunt Paula's hair was starting to turn gray. She *did* have a kind of a stripe in the middle of her head. Even with that, she looked beautiful—like Loretta Young or Elizabeth Taylor. She was that pretty. (And, if it's even possible, she was as sweet as my mother!)

My sister, who's eight years old, says, "Grandma, *I'm* Polish too!"

Grandma looks around to make sure no one's coming up the street, "Shhhhhh. We don't have to tell anyone."

See what I mean?

That kind of talk happened all my life. It puzzled me because my mother was Polish. She was beautiful and smart and kind, like my Babcia. Her Polish mother, Helen Ormanowski Bilski, was a smart business lady and gave my mother and father a whole house for a present—paid for! My Babcia gave all *three* of her children houses.

111

My father really liked my Babcia Bilski. To him, she was the best person. He was always happy when he was near her, and never said a bad thing about her. He *did* tell her that he didn't want her to speak Polish in front of us kids. That wasn't very nice, I admit.

But Grandma Aelish talked nasty about a lot of people and groups of people.

My father, her son, didn't say bad things. There was *one* exception: if someone hurt his children, he *did* give them a serious talking to. On *very* rare occasions, if he thought it was a good idea, he might do more.

As far as I know, he threatened to throw one guy, a mining supervisor, into a blast pit. The supervisor had OK'd a mining blast that resulted in my sister Olivia Marie being cut, and a bunch of cars damaged by huge balls of anthracite coal that fell, like hail, from the sky.

I read in the *Times Leader* the part about my father holding the guy over the huge open pit by the his shirt! In my father's defense, the mine company was blasting too close to the town, even though there was a regulation, saying not to do that.

All of this is leading up to the night I met Tommy Bassanelli.

Chapter 16

Tommy Bassanelli   1965

As Aunt Terry and I pass a house with a beautiful swimming pool in the backyard this amazingly cute boy comes walking out.

"Hi, Mrs. Jenkins. How are you?"

He doesn't look at me, but am I ever looking at him!

He's about 16, with black hair like Paul Anka's. I saw Paul Anka at a concert the summer before my mother died. I shocked myself with my own screaming and crying. That's how much I loved Paul Anka.

This boy is standing in front of us—awkward and embarrassed. But he doesn't move.

My Aunt smiles at him and says, "Tommy Bassanelli, this is my niece Katie Neumann. She's visiting me."

He turns, as if seeing me for the first time, "Hi."

I just look at his face, and his eyes, and think, "Wow."

"Maybe we can go swimming sometime," he says, and glances at his swimming pool. I shoot a quick look at Aunt Terry who's still smiling!

"Oh, that would be nice," even though I'm completely embarrassed because Aunt Terry is there. I'm not wearing my glasses, so I'm guessing he thinks I'm pretty. That thought gives me hope.

Then Tommy Bassanelli shocks me. *Shocks me*, by saying, "Do you think I could come over tonight, maybe about eight o'clock?" I'm shocked because he doesn't mean *sometime*. He means *tonight* at eight o'clock.

I have no idea what to say. This is the part of the story where my father would have said something that meant, "No."

Remember in *my* town, *my* family, we were only supposed to like Irish or Irish/German people, not Polish people (which my mother was) and definitely not Italian people, or Protestants. Bassanelli sounds Italian. Even so, Tommy looks so much like Paul Anka that I'm starting to hear "*Put Your Head on my Shoulder*."

When Paul Anka sang that song it was like he was singing right at me. Like he was saying, "I want *you* to be my girlfriend. I will hold you close and everything will be perfect."

I let my mouth just say whatever it wanted to say, which was, "OK."

I'm thinking, "I have no idea how to act on a real date. And, I'm thinking, "OK—even though I don't know if my father would have a fit because your name is Bassanelli."

You know how sometimes, your mind figures things out, like a bolt of lightning, before you know what's going on?

Well, with some quick computing, my mind does just that. I'm amazed to hear myself saying "OK," to an Italian boy asking me for a date.

My thinking goes like this: My father actually married a Polish person. So did his brother Steve (Aunt Paula's husband). So did his brother Raymond. Those aunts were terrific and beautiful. They turned out to be *very* good mothers.

And their husbands liked them.

By the way, no one ever tells you why you could like this one, but not *that* one. It's like being in a gang. You just had to like your gang but not someone else's gang or you'd be in instant trouble.

But here's Aunt Terry, who married Uncle Nigel, a Protestant, and she's smiling. So maybe an Italian boy would be a situation that people wouldn't mind.

Again, I think, "He looks exactly like Paul Anka." If I don't use self-control. I might start crying out of instant love, like I did at the concert!

Sure enough, on that very night at eight o'clock, Tommy Bassanelli shows up at my Aunt Terry and Uncle Nigel's door. I'm all dressed up and ready. He knows Uncle Nigel, whose entire face tells me he likes Tommy a lot.

There isn't even an embarrassing moment before we're out of the house. No burps from brothers. No "Isn't Katie beautiful?" from a father. No screaming from toddlers.

As Tommy and I are walking toward his house, I'm thinking he is so handsome, and nicer than anything.

Under my clothes I'm already wearing my bathing suit, ready for my first evening swim.

"How long will you be here?"

"Two more days."

"So, I guess, you're not dating anyone," he asks, already guessing the answer.

I want to blurt out, "I can't talk to you because you're really handsome ... and grown-up acting ... and I'm all mixed-up. The only thing I know how to do is babysit, and clean, and be smart in English class."

If I blurt it out, I might want to run screaming down the street. I manage to keep my thoughts to myself.

Just in case you're wondering about my problem with being mixed-up inside, it doesn't make sense to me either, because in school I'm really smart. These kinds of thoughts just pop up, like a bunch of gophers in a field.

But because, in my head, I keep hearing Paul Anka singing "Put Your Head on My Shoulder" and it gives me a very nice feeling, I make myself continue to act normal. Tommy's calm way of walking, and talking, makes this easier to pull off. I'm relieved that I'm not "going" with Eric Logan at the moment.

I ask, "What grade are you in?"

Inside, I think, "That's a dumb question."

I say to myself: "Think. Think of something more interesting, something that makes you sound cool." That idea works like a radio without a battery.

"Eleventh. And you?"

"Eleventh," I say.

Because Tommy seems more mature than I am, and kind, I find myself relaxing. I like him. I feel something else but can't put my finger on it. If I could put words to this feeling, I'd say, "Right now, I'm a normal girl who's having a date with a wonderful boy."

"Would you like to get some cola at my house?" he asks.

"That sounds great." I'm relieved that I'm acting like I'm comfortable being on a date.

At Tommy's, he introduces me to his mother.

"Mom, this is Katie Neumann. We're going swimming."

She nods but doesn't smile. I think maybe she doesn't like me because she's Italian and I'm Polish. That's all I can come up with that makes sense. It doesn't matter that I don't even know if she's Italian or Irish, or Hungarian.

The thought comes, "Nobody *said*, you're Polish. So she can't be crabby because of that."

Maybe she thinks it's rude for me to swim in her pool at night with a boy. She seems a little bit mad but doesn't try to stop us when we go out to the pool area with our cokes in hand.

"Is something wrong with your mother? Maybe she doesn't like you bringing a girl to the pool at night?"

"No, it's not that. My father died last year and I'm all she has. She's been acting that way ever since he died."

"I'm sorry. What happened?" I ask, not afraid to be in this territory.

117

His face looks so sad. "He died of a heart attack. Now it's just the three of us—me, my mother, and my younger brother. I try to watch out for him."

For the first time in years I don't feel annoyed ... or alone.

Without even thinking about it, I take my shorts off, then my blouse, glad that I own a decent looking bathing suit.

"Let's go in." He takes my hand, as if I'm special and he's guiding me into the water.

Almost out of nowhere, a feeling comes over me—I'm in an enchantment that's not ruined by a dark and dangerous magician—one who casts spells.

Tommy and I move together in the water. Not talking. Moving closer to the deep end of the pool.

He gently takes both of my hands. He smiles and swirls me around. I'm free. Completely free.

I hardly notice a sound coming from me. A soft, happy giggle. As if he doesn't need to think about it, he lifts me with both arms—holding me like a child. I'm a feather swirling through cool water, first faster, then more slowly.

Tommy's eyes and mine communicate perfectly: I'm a magical girl he found in a mysterious meadow. He's the boy who wants to hold me forever.

My arm moves around his neck, and I rest my head on his shoulder.

He's turning me more slowly, when I look up at him. That's when he kisses me. Without the tiniest hesitation, I kiss his soft, beautiful mouth, right back.

We stay there, in the water, kissing that way, for a long time.

And when we stop, we're both smiling, and laughing. We splash each other. Hold hands and kiss, a little bit more. When we come out, I dry my arms and legs. I let myself be washed over by this new feeling.

It feels special to be the girl who Tommy Bassanelli "likes." My world has changed, because I'm the girl who likes Tommy back. The feeling of the kiss doesn't leave, as we sit on the side of the pool holding hands. It doesn't leave, when later, I slip on my shorts and blouse and take his hand. Together—like two different people—we walk back to Aunt Terry's and Uncle Nigel's.

If you want to know what happened after that—nothing happened. I left to go back to school two days later. Before I left, Tommy asked me to come back in October to go to a high school dance.

I said, "Yes…"

But I didn't go.

The reason was, when I got back to my home in Allentown *real life* was waiting.

I felt like that night with Tommy Bassanelli, was a dream. My life at home was real. My responsibilities were real.

Almost overnight, I was scared, and angry. I worried if his friends saw me at the dance, they might say, "Why's Tommy with someone like *her*? He's so cute, and she's … she's strange."

When your mother dies and you're a teenager—you *are* strange. You don't do things that teenagers do. You don't laugh at things teenagers laugh at, or wear the clothes they do, or have the fun they do.

You stay home and "help out" a lot. You spend your free time being sad, or mad, or ... talking to angels. All of that starts showing up in the way you walk.

It shows up in the way you carry your books. The way you *have to* get out of normal teenage things. It shows up mostly in thoughts that don't make sense to anyone but you.

I started thinking, "If I went to the dance with Tommy, it would be a royal disaster."

I got out of the dance invitation by saying in a letter:

"I can't go to the dance with you because I found a new boyfriend who goes to my school."

If you think that's stupid and mean I do, too. But at least afterwards I felt relief, along with sadness.

I don't know why I didn't tell the truth: that I couldn't travel all the way back to New Jersey because I wouldn't be allowed. That I couldn't even ask to go because it would cause a problem at home.

I couldn't say the truth: that I felt stupid because I wouldn't fit in with his friends. That *they* would probably feel embarrassed, for Tommy, for taking me to the dance. That he would see me, then, the way his friends did.

That's all I know about telling that lie even though I knew it would hurt his feelings.

I'm trying, for the millionth time, to find the courage to open a letter that came two months ago from Tommy Bassanelli, a letter I received just three weeks after I wrote to him.

That I lied to him about having a new boyfriend, about not wanting to see him again, always made my head hurt.

When his letter came, I didn't open it.

I held it in my hands, almost every night—for weeks. Too many questions came out when I tried to make myself open his letter. Would he call me names? Would he call me a loser? Would he say that I hurt him when I told him—lied to him—that I had found another boyfriend?

Or worse I worried that he would be nice to me. That would even be harder to take—I knew that I had hurt the nicest boy a person could meet.

Almost every night, I held his letter in my hands and wished that I hadn't sent mine to him. I wished that I had been able to tell him the truth, the truth about being afraid that I would embarrass him by not being cool.

And then, on those nights, I would put it in a hiding place, under a loose floorboard in the back of my closet.

Chapter 17

A Light, Tiny as a Pin   1965

Mommy, it's been over a year since my angel's first visit. I've been doing better—knowing you're somehow part of me, even though you're not living here. From the night of my angel's last visit, it's been a little easier not having you in the world.

It's true...

our family has problems.

Not having you tucking the kids in, and making dinner, and singing in the car— is hard.

If I had to describe it, I'd say, "There's a hole in our family in the shape of YOU."

We're laughing just a bit more, and dancing more, like we used to. But there's a sadness, too.

Our aunts and uncles, and Daddy's and Eugenia's new friends say, "You're lucky to have Eugenia in your life." Even Daddy says that sometimes.

But if you're a kid who used to have YOU for a mother, you don't feel lucky.

There's something else ...

What my angel did last night was astonishing.

I mean… what WE (my angel and I) did last night is something that even you, might not ordinarily believe.

Except, you will. Because you were part of it!

Actually, because of last night, we're all going to be OK. Really OK!

This is the first time I could say that since the Good Friday in 1962 when you left us.

Right now, I can almost see you smiling, hear you saying, "Calm down," as if you're rocking a baby who's so wound up that she can't relax, can't even think straight.

Even though I'm definitely not a baby, it feels like you're saying, "There. There." It feels like you're holding me gently while you say it.

"There. There."

In my imagination I can see your soft, smiling eyes asking me, "Can you slow down a little? Start from the beginning. Tell me one small part of what happened, then the next, then the next. I'm not going anywhere. I'm right here with you."

In my own way, I DO hear you

I know that you're here with me.

So, here's the story, one small part at a time.

I'm asleep, dreaming ... I think. I really don't remember the dream except that I'm in a forest, that's dense and thick as tar. All I hear is a sad, crying sound, as if a lonely animal is calling out.

Even though I've never heard an actual wolf, I hear myself thinking, "A wolf's howling into the night."

Almost immediately, two things happen.

First, I realize that the wolf is hoping that someone will howl back.

Second, I wake up from the dream, realizing that there's a problem. Even though the wolf sound has gone, I'm still in the deepest part of the woods. Not in my bedroom, not asleep.

Just there, in the woods.

Awake.

That's when I notice that far ahead I see a light, tiny as a pin, and as absolutely bright as the forest is dark.

I don't need to think about what to do next.

Some part of me knows things in a new way, on this particular night, as if my brain has a new skill. If I believed in magic potions, which I don't, I would think that I just drank some.

Using this new skill, I know that the light isn't a star, or a lantern, or a night fire.

As sure as I know that you are my mother, I know that the light is my angel.

She's waiting for me just like you used to wait for me when you'd call Sherry Prymus's house after we played all day.

You'd say, "It's time to come home." And with every step from Sherry's home to mine, I'd know that you'd be there, waiting.

I know that I have to actually walk through the woods alone, to get to my angel. Yet, I have a feeling of— strength.

I'm not afraid at all.

Taking one step then another, I'm aware, in a wonderful way, of where the stones are. I don't stumble.

I know where every ditch is. I don't fall.

I know where the wild animal babies sleep for the night. I don't disturb them.

I walk one step at a time, through the black night, until my angel and I are only as far away as we always are when we talk in my bedroom.

"I knew you'd come tonight," my angel says.

I'm quiet, as if she's asked me to listen.

"After three years, you're still suffering. Your life with Eugenia, your father, and your brothers and sisters is still too hard. And yet, you keep trying to be a good girl. You go to mass even though you're very angry at God."

I'm nodding and noticing that the both of us are walking in these strange woods. To where, I have no idea.

If you were with me that night, you'd wonder how my angel knew all these things about what she called "my suffering."

I hadn't told her of many things that were going wrong: Not about Tommy Bassanelli and my big lie to him. Not about my brothers and sisters making fun of me for entering a beauty contest at Hess's Department Store.

I didn't say I'm crazy-scared of making big mistakes caring for my brothers and sisters. Having so much responsibility for Izzie—her being so little and all—is the most frightening of all.

If you were there that night, walking with my angel, you'd see the return of a long-ago memory, one that seemed to haunt me for years. It explained my conviction that I was not just a stupid big sister, but maybe, a bad person.

It started with an incident that occurred a very long time ago, when my sister Olivia Marie was only four years old. This was *before* our baby Izzie was even born—

when I still enjoyed being a mother's helper.

I was ten and had put some milk on the stove for hot chocolate for the kids. I went to the living room to give my mother *her* favorite drink—for when she was pregnant.

It was Alka-Seltzer with a big glass of water. She'd drink it down. Smile. And that was that! I'd take the empty glass back to the kitchen, happy that her stomach didn't hurt any more.

After giving my mother her drink, I turned to the doorway, on my way to the kitchen. There was Olivia Marie in the sweetest little dress, screaming.

Screaming!

I knew right away—her little hands curled up around her dress—that she had tried to reach up to see what was in the pot. That she spilled the scalding milk on her front.

I ran to her and pulled the dress off—right over her little head. Even though it was the fastest thing I ever did, it wasn't okay. ALL of the skin from a huge patch of her chest came off with the dress—Scalded off.

I'm not sure what happened then. I just remember that I was very stupid. That my little sister would have scars forever.

Like every other time I messed up (when my mother was alive) no one yelled at me. No one made me feel ashamed or punished me. I still knew whose fault the accident was.

That picture of Olivia Marie—the sweetest little girl in the world—in that doorway, screaming and running to me, with her little hands curled up, holding her dress (melting where the milk spilled), never went away.

From that one day, I had all the evidence I needed to know that only a careless sister, a horrible sister, would let that happen.

If the angel knew any of these things, she didn't say. Just seeing her, moving—steady and focused—seemed to pull me away from these old memories and back to the present.

"Where are we going," I asked.

"You'll know soon enough," she said.

I walked, one foot in front of the other, behind her. I noticed then, that she seemed to glide and she seemed to glow. If I poked her back with my finger (not that I would) it would go right through her. I was so used to my angel now that her gliding and glowing didn't bother me.

If you were with us that night, you'd know that she and I were on a mission more important than any before. You'd remember that, for me, most normal things had lost their importance: Going to a prom. Buying new clothes. Being popular. And doing things with friends.

This night was different.

Chapter 18

The Mythmaker   1965

After walking for a very long time, the angel and I stop on a high ridge.

Looking down, I'm surprised to see a shoreline far below. Something catches my eye: A long stretch of white sand where the land meets a sapphire sea.

As if this night isn't strange enough, I notice that some deep mystery seems to open. I hear soft waves falling in a rhythm as old as time, and wonder, "could all of this be too splendid for the normal world?"

A woman, bent low to the ground, works quietly.

I think, "Maybe she's an artist holding her crooked stick like a brush." She seems to have just finished writing in the sand.

Straining to make out each letter, I see words, not quite understandable to me.

I begin reading out loud, hoping that if I hear it, the message will make some sense to me:

"The mythmaker writes your name."

As I'm puzzling over these strange words, I notice a rising sun, brilliant and bold. As if a movie scene has shifted from one world to another, a single-masted ship appears from behind the sun.

With lightning speed, it rises—high in the sky.

For what seems like a long time, the ship glides effortlessly through empty air toward the land below. With only one small course correction, this unmanned vessel steers toward the woman.

Finally, it rests on solid ground—not far from the strange message in the sand. Inches from the woman.

I'm not sure what I expect, but as she silently boards the ship with the grace of a swan, I'm not at all surprised.

I watch her standing on deck. My singular thought is, "I wonder. Is this why I'm here—to see her?"

In this very moment, her head tilts toward where I stand with my angel on the high ledge above. The woman smiles as if she knows me.

Without the slightest warning from the sea, quiet as a new dawn—

an ocean wave erupts. It carries the ship, with the woman—standing tall and unafraid—to the cliff, to my angel, and to me.

She leaves the ship and begins to walk, as there's still a short distance between us.

Each small step brings her features a bit more into focus.

I see, at first, a surprising resemblance to my own mother.

This doesn't shock me, because all along I've been seeing or hearing my mother in coffee shops, and church, and even pizza parlors. A hundred times, I've gotten so excited so hopeful. My heart skips with new and amazing joy.

In the past, I've thought the woman in the coffee shop (who I might see from behind) is *her*.

"That's definitely my mother's silhouette, her way of sitting, of bending her head. She seems to have my mother's hair."

I would wonder, "Isn't that her favorite sweater? The one she so often wore to Bingo?"

My spirits would lift, for a few seconds—only to find, that it was only another trick of hope, or longing. It was as if, in that important moment, some mysterious world order thought that my need for my mother was nothing.

Always, the woman was *not* her.

Upon a closer look, the woman in the coffee shop was not even *like* her. I would be disappointed every time, in a completely new way.

As if on a rollercoaster, I would think, "Oh, she's alive!"

Then, "No, she's dead."

Even since my angel started being with me, this thinking, this hoping, that my mother is in the world, then knowing she isn't … still hurts.

But this is different. This woman comes closer, and closer still. I see more of her. This isn't a trick, not a stranger at all.

This *is* my mother.

MY MOTHER.

I wonder, will she take me to board the ship? In that same moment, it's as if she is touching my hand, drawing me to her.

It's then, that even more unimaginable events occur, each with a dizzying acceleration, and me, feeling that I might not be able to keep up.

We are like light itself, my mother and I.

Suddenly we are deep under the ocean's currents, close to a richly-colored coral reef.

Luminescent creatures swim past, as my mother and I remain in what I'll say is ... a place of many places—all at the same time.

As if by magic, in an instant we find ourselves among millions of stars in the night sky, belonging in a way I've never imagined.

We are everywhere at once: below, above, here, and also there. No longer bound by normal rules of time or place. It's all so wonderful that I'm not afraid, not even confused. How could I be? I'm with my beautiful mother, my mother who is no longer lost to me.

Turning, I look far below and see my angel. She nods me forward, signaling to me that I belong with my mother ... at least for now.

That may be the moment when a first sound comes from my mother, like a tingle of chimes in the early morning. But then, I realize that it's not so much a sound as a feeling, coming from her to me. Right now, there are no words, only wonder.

Both of our hearts are completely full with what has quickly become the undeniable sound of *our* laughter. And in the same space, there is also a warmth and quiet.

A *new* feeling is everywhere—chasing all loneliness away, all resentment, all anger, all loss.

If you've ever seen a sunrise—a sun bursting from behind a mountain—you know this feeling. The opposite of darkness, of ... loneliness.

Now, I'm in the light of this radiant sun.

There isn't a "me," or a "she," but instead, a kind of union.

What's completely true right now, is that my mother never died. She never fell off a mountain—leaving me alone on a dangerous ledge, without her.

And then, everything changes.

As quickly as the flap of a butterfly's wing, her presence brings me back to the place where my angel waits.

If you were there, you'd be stunned. And still, something even more fantastic happens.

My mother reaches to me and caresses me. *All* of me. She is, for one moment, flesh and blood—warm, soft, tender, no longer an image, no longer just light and joy.

135

Out of her mouth come real words, the kind of words I can hear, the kind anyone can hear.

She says, "You're my sweet child. I'll be here with you, in your heart, until you're completely grown, until your brothers and sisters are grown. Only then will I go to my *new* home."

"Where will you go?" I ask, aware that I can ask her anything I want, but afraid too, because she mentioned leaving me.

"To the home another has prepared for me."

She isn't quite finished. "It's there that I will prepare a home for you and for your brothers and sisters. They're my sweet babies, too. That's my promise to each of you."

As if I knew that our conversation might come to an end before I could ask another question, I said, "Wait!"

Seemingly knowing exactly what I would ask next, she stands still as a tree rooted in the ground.

"Mother, who is the mythmaker?"

"Oh," she asks, "my words in the sand?"

I nod.

Once more, I hear that sound, the one reminding me of soft wind chimes. After the briefest of pauses she says, "*You are.*"

And seeing my puzzled expression, she patiently continues, "When the time is right, my precious child, you will tell your story. It will be deepened by time and wisdom and the magic of the heart. It will be *your* story, and also mine, and your angel's story."

She continued, "Your myth is the remembering of this deep and clear time with me, and importantly, of all the loss and sorrow before. Think of it as putting together something that has been lost or broken, just as my death broke all of your lives.

Re-membering means putting back all that life dis-membered. Re-membering will make life whole again—more special than it was before."

I'm nodding now, more to encourage her to continue speaking, than to show her that I understand.

She continues, "And still, my precious child, myth is bigger than any one truth. Larger than memory. Your mythmaking will also write the name of Life and Death itself. Your words will show the patterns within this deep mystery."

"Because you are a mythmaker, your story, indeed, *our* story, will be one that everyone can hear."

"Everyone?" I ask.

"Yes, for all of those with ears to hear," she says.

"Like all myth, yours will allow the stories of our family—of many families— to cohere."

Seeing confusion on my face, she explains, "Events—like beads strung together by a jeweler's careful hand—connect, creating a wondrous whole. *This* is coherence."

She goes on, "You think our family tragedy exists by itself—an explosion, throwing our lives asunder? That is only part of the truth. Our family tragedy is one of *many* mysteries that tell our story past and present."

137

A tear falls from my eye as I say, "I don't think I'll know how to be a mythmaker."

With a warm finger wiping away the tear, she asks, "Do you trust me?"

"Always," I answer.

"Then you can be at peace with all of this."

"You must only concern yourself with living your life in the best way possible—to be the best sister you can be, to go to school, and even to dances. You'll read that letter from that nice boy, the letter you keep hidden."

"After many years, after growing into yourself, you will know what to say. You will know *how* to say it. For you, being a mythmaker will bring you and others joy."

"I wonder how you can know all this?" I whisper.

Her answer made sense to me, "Just like I knew you were coming today. Just like I knew to write the message in the sand."

Smiling, she told me, "Only mythmakers see angels. There are so many where I'm going. There, they are known as Divine messengers. They too, can see with the heart."

As if she wanted to make sure I understood the most important part of her message, she said, "You will always know, somewhere deep inside, what we did here today, together."

"What if I forget?"

"Everyone forgets enchantments, for a time. For *you*, there will be a sign to bring the memory of our time together back into being. This will remind you that *you* are free now to experience the joy that other young people experience."

"This sign will reveal itself tomorrow and will help you remember—until you're ready to fulfill your role."

She continues, "Tomorrow, when you are home, when you dress Olivia Marie for school, pay attention. Olivia Marie—the sister you always say is so sweet, so dear to your heart—will no longer be scarred."

"What will remain will be a faint pink color, as pleasant as a young girl's rosy cheek. Without her scar, there's no longer a reason to hold yourself at fault."

Looking at me, she almost whispers, "Faultfinding … diminishes all of us. Even the ten-year-old girl within you, who left a little sister unattended, not knowing that she would scald herself."

"Your touchstone is your freedom from blame," she says.

"Before I leave, I want to give you this …"

With a downcast glance, she directs my gaze to a box cradled in the palm of her hand.

Hardly breathing, I ask, "Is this the box my angel brought on the night I first met her?"

Nodding, she says, "You can trust this gift from *me*.

The terror of that first night, the paralysis, the running as if on a moving barrel—all come back with the power of a sorcerer's spell. I'm immobile, suddenly grounded in midair.

Seeing my hesitation, my mother encourages, "You were a different girl then, so afraid of a reality you didn't understand. Go ahead. Open it. "

Ever so cautiously, I reach for the box and remove the lid. Inside ... a globe glows. Its soft light ebbs and flows, responding to a secret rhythm. Reaching in to hold it closer, I'm aware only of my mother's love; the fear of receiving a gift from a ghost in the dark of night is as far away as a distant galaxy.

No longer surprised by anything this wondrous night brings, I gaze at what seems to be a miniature, three-dimensional scene of a living world.

"That's the grotto I used to play in when I was little," I say.

Leaning closer to me, my mother whispers, "Look deeper."

I see two women seated at a table. They're sitting opposite each other in a diner. I'm dumbfounded.

I say, "But ... that's the Ham Fam."

My mother giggles, "Yes, it's the Hamilton Family Diner. You take Eugenia there for lunch one afternoon after Daddy's with me."

It's then that I realize that the two women are old— Eugenia, and a grownup me. The surprise of this makes the words," after Daddy's with me," move to the back of my mind ... for now.

My mother says, "For me, there's no longer a past or a future. Everything can be seen in the present. I wanted to share this with you."

I'm following my mother's lead. We tilt our heads toward the globe, close enough to hear.

Eugenia speaks first. "I wish I'd been kinder to John's children."

I wonder, "Does she know that *I'm* one of John's children?"

Though *that* question seems unimportant.

I'm noticing that I can *feel* exactly what the grown Katie feels. To my disbelief, it isn't anything like what you would expect. Instead of hate or meanness, there's something else entirely.

It's tenderness ... I think.

"And compassion," my mother adds. Again, I've forgotten how easily she, like my angel, knows my feelings, my thoughts.

In response to Eugenia's comment, *grown* me says, "I think ... when we face our failings, we become more human."

My eyes pop wide open as I notice the grown-up *me* reach across the table and take Eugenia's hand.

Looking at this— I'm speechless.

Turning to my mother, I see the tiniest trace of amusement. "You don't need to know everything that lies ahead for you. But the moment *will* come, when a grownup you encounters Eugenia as an old woman. It's only at that time, that a vulnerable heart will open within *her*."

"You'll respond exactly as I've shown you," she says.

"Your kindness towards her will be part of *your* healing."

I lower my eyes then, knowing she's heard my words days before, threatening to cut Eugenia with a knife.

I feel the warmth of her touch as she raises my face just a bit. The gesture allows my eyes to meet hers. I see pure love.

"*We* don't do things like *that* in our family," she says. "*You* don't do things like that."

"You always were—always are—*my* Katie."

With one final caress, she seems to slowly disappear. Never taking her eyes from mine, until she is no more.

With the last part of my mother's message completed, my angel accompanies me home.

Author's Note

I wrote this story so that young people who experience the death of a parent, as I did, might feel less alone and more understood. From the outside, children who experience such a loss may seem OK. They may appear to be resilient, healed, happy, or coping well. But often, their inner life is one of grief and confusion. What they need from those who care about them is authentic assistance in mourning.

Mourning is a process that moves grief from an inner experience to an outer one. Alan Wolfelt, Ph.D., a respected leader in the field of grief counseling, tells us that it is through this outer, shared experience that healing happens. We mourn as we find a way to remember, in the company of others, our parent. We might do this through recollections, or metaphoric activities: creating a memory album, or filling a jar with tender sayings or objects that honor the deceased.

The kind of metaphoric knowing found in *The Mythmaker* is also an appropriate expression of loss and resolved grief, and a way to re-member a life dismembered by unacceptable loss. Katie's story demonstrates that personal myth can also connect the past with the present, as well as the material with the nonphysical world. When others in our lives provide support and a willingness to listen, recollections and remembering become shared experiences, and healing moves forward. Without others to carefully listen our grief can become stuck inside.

The last two chapters of *The Mythmaker* are a metaphor for the healing that occurred in my life. What did happen in the concrete world? Over many years, and through my work with several excellent therapists, I mourned until I healed. I was able to learn the women's mysteries that my mother's death took from me. My mother would have used her wisdom to help me navigate my life as an adolescent girl and a young woman. Had she been at my side, I could have learned what I needed to know about life in a matter of years instead of decades. And it is true that after the passage of those decades I did find a way to reconnect with my precious mother, in the way of the heart.

I did indeed experience an angel who came to me many months after my mother died. But unlike brave Katie in my story, I was afraid to speak with her. Writing *The Mythmaker* was my act of imagining what my angel and I might have said to each other if I talked with her, instead of allowing my fear to keep both of us silent.

I also wrote *The Mythmaker* to highlight some of the inner conflicts and feelings that a child might experience when a parent dies. For me, there was unspoken isolation and anger, and unreasonable shame and jealousy. Surprisingly, I was not aware of these feelings until much later in life when I had some distance from my loss. On the outside I was a perfect child, a helper, and a big sister. I smiled readily and no one knew the depth of my loss. Often, when a child or a young adult loses a parent, he or she experiences anxiety that is so persistent, and so deep that it becomes a part of personality, and often goes unnoticed by both the child, and her family. Sometimes, the response to the loss of a parent is negative or destructive behavior. What's important to know is that there's no map for this territory called parent loss.

I encourage all of my readers who have experienced the early death of a parent to accept all feelings as legitimate, and all timelines as personal paths, deserving neither judgment, nor grievance. I encourage you, when you are ready, to create rituals in which you remember the life of your parent, and your precious place as a son or daughter. Use your imagination to do this, even if your parent had flaws. Do this, because the deepest part of our being understands ritual in a way that the rational mind does not. Our deepest self allows rituals to transform suffering into healing, and loss into reconnection.

As two examples, I share the following accounts. First, a friend of mine who lost a brother early in life, gathers with her family on his birthday. During the celebration the family eats the dishes that their brother and son most enjoyed, and tell loving stories about him. This friend is Dr. Kim Bateman who wrote a wonderful book on healing the loss of a love called *Crossing the Owl's Bridge: A Guide for Grieving People Who Still Love* (Chiron Publications, 2016).

And a second example of ritual reconnection: many years after our mother's death, my older sister JoAnn found our mother's recipe for her legendary chocolate cake. For our younger sister's 60th birthday, JoAnn placed the recipe in a frame and included a poem JoAnn wrote. The poem made our younger sister know that our mother delights in her; that our mother would be so pleased at the person she has become. In this imaginal way, our mother was symbolically present at a birthday party that occurred many decades after her passing. In the early years after my mother's death, I would have thought such things were pointless responses to the unacceptable loss of someone so lovely, someone so necessary to our family. But now, I understand that such imaginative connection is a gift.

As my friend Dennis Patrick Slattery, author of *Riting Myth, Mythic Writing: Plotting Your Personal Story* (Fisher King Press, 2012), has taught me, our personal myths are the threads that make our lives cohere. To the world they may be fictions, but to our souls they are transforming potions.

About the Author

Dr. Mary Harrell is a Jungian-oriented psychotherapist, author, and poet. She is an Associate Professor Emeritus at State University of New York (SUNY) at Oswego. Dr. Harrell practices clinical psychology through teletherapy in New York and offers private Jungian seminars worldwide. Mary's interest in imaginal psychology has led her to investigate the way in which archetypal patterns manifest in experience. In addition to *The Mythmaker*, she is the author of *Imaginal Figures in Everyday Life: Stories from the World between Matter and Mind* (Chiron Publications, 2015). She lives with her husband Stephen in South Carolina and can be reached at maryharrellphd.com and themythmaker.com.

Timothy Teague Photography

CPSIA information can be obtained
at www.ICGtesting.com
Printed in the USA
LVHW03s2127060718
582980LV00001B/5/P

9 781630 515003